CUT TO THE

BONE

2

CUT TO THE
BONE

ROBERT CONNER

alyson books
los angeles | new york

MANUFACTURED IN THE UNITED STATES OF AMERICA.

THIS TRADE PAPERBACK ORIGINAL IS PUBLISHED BY ALYSON PUBLICATIONS,
P.O. BOX 4371, LOS ANGELES, CALIFORNIA 90078-4371.
DISTRIBUTION IN THE UNITED KINGDOM BY TURNAROUND PUBLISHER SERVICES LTD.,
UNIT 3, OLYMPIA TRADING ESTATE, COBURG ROAD, WOOD GREEN,
LONDON N22 6TZ ENGLAND.

FIRST EDITION: NOVEMBER 2002

02 03 04 05 06 **a** 10 9 8 7 6 5 4 3 2 1

ISBN 1-55583-695-X

LIBRARY OF CONGRESS CATALOGING-IN-PUBLICATION DATA
   CONNER, ROBERT, 1947–
     ISBN 1-55583-695-X
      1. EL PASO (TEX.)—FICTION. 2. DRUG TRAFFIC—FICTION. 3. HATE CRIMES—
FICTION. 4. GAY MEN—FICTION. I. TITLE.
PS3603.O63 C87 2002
   813'.6—DC21   2002074599

CREDITS
• COVER PHOTOGRAPHY FROM PHOTODISC.
• COVER DESIGN BY LOUIS MANDRAPILIAS.

CUT TO THE
BONE

S o this *estúpido,* this bastard motherfuck, dickless dog-fuck stupid *mierda* piece of shit *ése, hijo de la chingada...*he hands the shipment over to them. *Así, no más,* after we've paid this *menso hijo de nadie* over 200 big...*con una chinga-da...*200 big in just one year, goddamn it...which is more than this goddamn *pinche* shit-hole *alevoso* cop makes in...what? Ten years? To wave a couple of *pinche* trucks in *mano, no más...*after his dog-fuck *puta* whore of a wife buys a cabin and 10 acres in Cloudcroft! I'm telling you, *mano...*I cannot fucking believe how goddamn stupid these ass-wipes in the border patrol are!" The fat man looked around in frustration, as if expecting one of the waiters to hold up a sign or something with the answer to just how stupid the ass-wipes in the border patrol could be.

Santos passed his right hand along the side of his head, down to the nape and back up to the crown, up and down a couple of times through the bristles of his hair.

The purple flush on Gregorio's puffy face faded slowly to a more restful crimson. "I'm telling you, *mano,* these motherfuckers are going to cause me to stroke."

Santos nodded compassion, relieved he didn't have the fat man's job. Middle management. What a bitch. He stretched his legs and stared for a while at the silver tips of his boots without saying anything.

Stupidity. The unforgivable sin. The *only* sin, to tell the truth. Never to be pardoned, not in this world nor in the world to come. Greed, treachery, blowing your cool at the check-points, not having your papers in order, playing both ends against the middle, cutting yourself a piece: Yes, there were a hundred ways of being stupid for every one way of being smart. But losing a shipment? Now *that* was the ultimate stupidity. Losing a shipment demanded exemplary punishment, a very public auto-da-fé, so the less afflicted might be warned off by the ostentatious sufferings of the hopelessly lost.

Santos, one of the avenging angels of this moral order, knew that when Gregorio Olivares turned a deathly shade of purple and ranted about stupidity, retribution had taken wing. And upon whom would fall its cruel talons? Santos waited to hear.

"So, anyway, they're going up to their cabin this weekend. The stupid fucks. So flush that goddamned shit, all right? And burn that fucking cabin of theirs down on them." Gregorio dumped pico de gallo on his fajitas and, regaining his com-posure, rolled the savory beef into the pillowy softness of a flour tortilla. So Friday would be ass-wipe payback day. Come Friday night, another stupid fuck would exit the world the way the stupid always had and always would. Compared to the millions they'd lost, the cop and his fucking cabin meant nothing, *nada en absoluto*. Still, it was the principle of the thing. Gregorio's fat-swaddled eyes fixed on Santos with a feral peasant cunning that far surpassed mere intelligence. "This *pinche hijo de la vecina* thinks he can fuck us over!" The fat man emitted a snort of derision at the very idea. "So do it this weekend, OK?"

"*Cierto, no hay pedo*. No problem at all." Santos popped

his neck, leaned back a little in his chair, and squeezed the juice of two lime slices into his Corona. Mexican *limonada*. He straightened his right arm, savoring the twinge of pain. The orthopedist called it "tennis elbow," and had explained that it was a small tear at the origin of some obscure forearm muscle. Santos, who didn't care dick one way or another about some game like tennis, knew he'd picked it up doing biceps curls with a straight bar. He decided he'd take a week off and then switch back to the EZ curl bar. Much easier on the elbows.

"*Bueno.* So fuck those assholes over good." Gregorio's dimpled hand, the hand of an enormous fallen cherub, proffered an equally fat envelope secured with a rubber band. For the next hour they ate and told war stories and jokes. Neither mentioned anything more about *migra* sellouts, or about the violation of the line release that until a few days ago had let the cartel's tanker trucks cross the frontier without the border patrol agents inspecting the contents. From time to time, Gregorio sneaked envious looks at Santos's arms, and Santos pretended not to notice.

] ✶ [

The wheels of the antique Jeep skittered slightly and the frame rattled as Santos crossed the abandoned tracks on Santa Fe. He jammed the shift into third and popped the clutch. The Jeep lurched forward. Empty brick warehouses blurred by on the right. Rusting railways splayed away into the darkness on the left. A block before Santa Fe turned east under the bridge, he slowed, guided the vehicle into the $3 lot and parked nose out, facing the side street.

"Not as cold tonight," he said, thumbing through bills in search of three ones.

"Thank God. I nearly froze myself out here Tuesday night." The woman's soiled hands added his dollars to a folded stack, stuck the wad into her change belt, and pulled her ratty coat over it.

Over the last couple of years their ritual had varied only once. For a few months after the woman's husband had been hit by a runaway truck while tending the parking lot, Santos had regularly inquired about his progress, but merely as a courtesy. He didn't even know their names. Tonight the ritual ended as it always did: "Have fun, be careful, and get drunk!" she called out after him. He replied with a short wave, not bothering to turn. Some day, he thought, he would perform this ritual for the last time and leave Mexico behind forever. But not tonight.

The breeze picked up as he entered the small plaza at the base of the bridge, lifting trash and dead mulberry leaves into knee-high swirls. The *teporochos* had deserted the iron benches, having migrated to wherever it was winos went when the weather turned cold. An empty whiskey bottle clattered loudly across the broken pavement as a gust of wind spun it toward the gutter.

At the bottom of the bridge, anonymous brown hands collected another of his dollars and pushed three quarters in change back through the tiny window of the toll booth. His pace slowed as he ascended the crest of the bridge. At the summit, where sun-bleached American and Mexican flags snapped in the wind, he paused, as he always did, and gazed back at the cluster of banks and hotels on the American side, then toward the illuminated star on the Franklin mountains. First Vegas, now El Paso. He'd long since tired of seared, dusty cities stuck in the middle of endless deserts. He needed to do a deal, a real one, and move away to some place green and cool. Away from all this drought and desperation.

Santos sighed and turned forward again, down the Mexican side of the bridge, toward the strip of seedy discos and curio shops along Avenida Juárez. Uglier than two boils on the ass of the Baby Jesus by day, by night the sister cities transformed themselves into a vast glittering ocean of sequined lights.

Below him, the soiled waters of the Rio Grande coursed silently in their concrete sluice. Except for a couple crossing on the other side, the bridge appeared deserted. He walked through the Mexican customs checkpoint uninspected. The two *aduaneros* on duty perched on a chairless metal desk inside the drafty station, warming themselves over a portable space heater, ignoring the occasional pedestrian. Descending the steps from the *aduana*, he crossed the street and slipped between the clumps of hookers and *cholos* outside the discotheques and bars, threading his way through their mostly underage patrons.

"*Oye, compa*, you wanna to see the girls? Donkey show!"

Santos smiled at the man and shook his head.

"Cheaper than Kmart!" the man shouted after him.

Santos tried to imagine a donkey show at Kmart. A Mexican Kmart with red light specials. He could almost see it.

He eased forward through the throngs of gangbangers and their teenage-girl skank, mentally picking out the boys he liked. He imagined what they would be like stripped: sensuous *mestizo* lips, sinuous limbs, lean asses with a smell like wood smoke. "If you're not thinking about sex, your mind's wandering," had been his uncle Vito's most frequent observation on life.

"Taxi, mister? Young girls!" another man called. A sex bazaar with certified virgins for sale. Guaranteed unscrewed and cheaper than Kmart.

Mexicans. Even their writers called them *los hijos de la*

chingada. Sons of the fucked woman. Half the cab drivers here were pimps, receiving a percentage for each customer dropped at the whorehouses of Boystown. Homeless kids washed car windows in the snarled traffic, juggled balls at intersections, and breathed fire for bored motorists. Store clerks made the equivalent of $20 American per week, with the cost of shoplifted merchandise deducted from their pay. The brutal Federal Judicial Police drove SUVs stolen from American tourists. *Fayuqueros* smuggled TVs in from the U.S. to avoid duty and stocked entire stores with them. Forty percent of the population younger than 14, drugs the leading export, houses with no running water, sleeping three and four to a room, corruption the oldest national institution. Santos figured anybody who couldn't do business in a shit-hole like this couldn't give away Popsicles in hell.

He walked down three blocks, cut through the remainder of a crippled Pemex station with truncated concrete stubs where the pumps had been, and crossed the street to the Club Lite. He passed three dollars to the doorman with the cannonball shoulders, and was waved in. He checked his jacket. The acne-scarred kid behind the counter appraised its supple black leather and smiled his availability as Santos paid him two dollars not to steal his coat.

Busy for a Thursday, he thought as he entered. A gaggle of men stood at the base of an elevated platform and stared up the groove of the perfect ass of a gyrating boy wearing only cowboy boots and butt floss.

"*Buenas noches, amigo.*" Santos handed the waiter five ones for a Corona, and added a friendly squeeze on the arm as he moved slowly toward the back of the bar, checking out the crowd. Heads turned to watch as he edged his way along the narrow strip of floor between the men lining the bar and the raised dance floor heaving with couples. So far no one here attracted him except the stripper on his pedestal, but Santos was not the kind who paid. The waiter approached, a cold bottle of beer and three ones riding his small round tray. "*Quédese con el resto*," Santos said as he accepted the beer. The waiter tipped his head in appreciation and smiled complicity. Locals called the strip and its environs "*el silencio*" because no one talked about who they saw here or what they'd seen them doing. City officials preferred to call it "*la zona de tolerancia.*"

All the tiny tables were loaded with bottles, glasses, and ashtrays overrun with stubbed-out butts. Santos leaned against a narrow column and avoided the persistent gaze of one of the local *vaqueros*. Unless they were tall and slender, the cowboys didn't interest him. The one now staring at him relentlessly was a pudgy pockmarked troll in cowboy drag. His eyes moved back to the dancing boy, down his smooth chest, and followed the trickle of dark hair from his navel to where the stream widened at the top of his thong. The boy hooked his thumb into the cloth pouch and eased the fabric down just enough to give the crowd a glimpse of his cock. At that moment the song changed. The dancing boy gracefully dismounted his platform, snatched up the shirt he'd let fall to the floor, and threaded his arms into the sleeves. With a disdainful toss of his head he headed back toward the dressing room, ignoring the people he passed. A few couples stepped down from the dance floor, replaced by more couples. Someone brushed his arm lightly but quite deliberately as he passed.

Santos turned.

The young man was tall enough to meet his gaze directly with eyes that simultaneously challenged and promised. He walked a short distance away and stopped, maintaining eye contact with Santos. And Santos watched him. A shorter youth hurried over to the young man and excitedly whispered some *chisme* in his ear, but he waved his friend away, never looking away from Santos. Santos nodded slightly and the boy smiled back, with an old man's eyes and a girl's mouth, the teeth white and perfect.

Santos edged his way toward him through the smoke and conversation. "Would you like to dance?" he asked.

"*Sí, cierto,*" the boy replied, still smiling. Santos slipped an arm around his slender waist and guided him through the crowd, toward the mirrored wall at the back of the dance floor, pulling him close as other couples moved into the space around them. With their gentle collision, Santos felt the heat of his partner's rising sex and the hunger for mutual possession.

"My name is Antonio," the boy said in accented English.

"*Mucho gusto*, Antonio. My friends call me Santos."

"You can call me Tony," the younger man replied. Santos's hand moved up Tony's spine, traced the back where it gently flared, circled a shoulder that was lean but not gaunt. Tony's fingertips followed a vein up Santos's arm and lingered to explore the splay of his triceps. Santos drew him into full contact, and nuzzled him under the ear. The boy put his arms around him and laid his head against his neck. Fully aroused, he pressed his pelvis hard against Santos. They pretended to dance for a while before leaving together.

| ✭ |

The next night, Friday, Santos drove his rental car north through New Mexico to Cloudcroft, arriving well after dark. He checked his directions repeatedly before pulling off the darkened road next to a spacious cabin. Light shone from the back windows, painting soft yellow rectangles on the pale blue snow. Wisps of smoke rose from the stone chimney, straight up into the branches of the towering pines. Next to the cabin sat a late-model Ford pickup. Santos stood in the icy driveway long enough to verify the number on the truck's Texas plates. Satisfied that he'd found the correct address, he mounted the steps to the porch.

The screen door was ajar. The owners had left it unhooked. Up here at the ski resort, far from the sin of the city streets, even a cop's sense of security got lax. Santos pushed the door back firmly against the jamb and knocked. He waited a few moments and knocked again, snuggling his thick woolen scarf up to protect his ears. A light came on in the front room. A man with the bored, sagging expression worn by all career border patrol officers turned on the porch light and peered through the glass. As the door opened, the cabin exhaled a warm gust of stale cigarette odor into the cold air.

"Hi," Santos said. "Listen, I'm sorry to disturb you like this, but I'm moving in a couple of doors down"—he pointed down the hill in the direction of the other cabins—"and my wife's just gotten really sick. We don't have a phone yet, and I was wondering if you'd let me make a call from here?"

"Sure. No problem. Come on in." The mark's belly dangled over the top of his pants, stretching the flimsy gray material of his undershirt. *Ten gallons of shit in a one gallon sack,* Santos thought. He scraped the snow from the heavily grooved soles of his leather hiking shoes while the man held the screen door open and stepped back to let him in.

"Thanks," he murmured. "I'll only take a minute." Santos kicked him hard under the left knee cap, lifting the patella off the underlying bone. The man gasped and doubled over, speechless with surprise and pain. Santos slammed his right knee up into his chin as he stumbled forward, snapping his head backward. The cop's body folded to the wooden floor with a heavy thud. Santos stepped over its inert bulk into the cabin's living area, slipping a short, hooked blade from the pocket of his coat. From a room in the back, dishes clattered and a woman's voice called out, "Honey, shut the door for Christ's sake, will ya?! You're gonna freeze us to death!"

| ✳ |

Over the course of the next week, six bodies surfaced in Juárez. Two, belonging to a ranking police officer and his oldest son, had been studiously mutilated, desexed, and stuffed into the trunk of the officer's car. Another, of a woman, her face mostly missing, was spotted by children playing on the bank of a sewage ditch. The medical examiner eventually identified her using the serial numbers on her breast implants. The other three corpses, which were never claimed or identified, were buried as paupers in unmarked graves.

The charred remains of the border patrolman and his wife, sifted from the ashes of their cabin, were positively identified from dental radiographs. Their subpoenaed bank records revealed substantial periodic infusions of cash, and family and friends emerged to testify to a spate of lavish purchases, wondering, but only in retrospect, it seemed, how a lowly border patrol officer and his secretary wife had managed to live so high on the hog. But of their killer, no clue remained apart from some tracks made by a common brand of tire.

Following these discoveries, EPIC, the El Paso Intelligence Center, nestled in the safety of Fort Bliss, was reorganized, and its previous director transferred. The new director, an earnest Mormon pit bull known to suffer from chronic moral priapism, reassigned the key positions to his younger puppies. But in spite of the reorganization and increased surveillance, the cartel's tanker fleet rolled unimpeded through the border checkpoints. No further shipments were lost. The amount of cartel cash moving through El Paso banks increased to nearly $150 million per month, up 30% over the previous year. The banks, in turn, loaned out the laundered funds for new homes, restaurants, and boutiques, which sprang up like desert wildflowers on the city's affluent west side and the leafy streets of the walled communities of the Upper Valley. The stupid had again been vanquished, the Pax Mexicana tentatively restored.

Santos invested half the contents of his fat envelope in high-yield biotech stocks, maintained his connections, made love to Antonio enthusiastically and often, and went daily to the gym while he waited for the mighty wheel of commerce to turn its inevitable round.

CHAPTER TWO

Since Chuy Acevedo had gotten his new *gringa* partner, the guys at Central had never let up. Not for a minute. How did he like being part of the bitch team? Had he dunked her doughnut? Very fucking funny. Chuy had tried not to let on how much he hated being paired with a woman, but he guessed it showed anyway. Women had no place in law enforcement beyond dispatch. Anybody with any brains had to know that.

"Yo, Acevedo! Can I borrow your lipstick?" The taunting voice behind him belonged to Jeff Thurmond, one of the night-shift fucks. Acevedo buried his head in his locker, determined to ignore him. "Hey...Detective Maxipad! I'm talking to you, sweet-lips!" the voice said, even louder.

Male laughter erupted throughout the locker room.

Acevedo shut his locker door very quietly and turned toward Thurmond, who stood staring at Acevedo with his usual stupid grin spread across his wide face. Several other men had gathered behind him, curious to see Acevedo's reaction.

Keeping his face blank, Acevedo walked up to the taller man without a word and shoved him hard in the chest. Thurmond, clearly expecting a verbal response, went sprawling backward over the bench between the rows of lockers and landed against them with a crash. Acevedo, who had taught CQC—close quarters combat—at the police academy long before Thurmond's time, waited quietly for him to get up.

More laughter erupted, with an even more sarcastic edge this time, now that the joke was on Thurmond.

When the big man got up, Chuy noted with satisfaction that there was murder in his eyes.

"You fuckin' greaseball," Thurmond spit, reaching a beefy hand to grab Acevedo's shirt. The grab almost made it, but not quite. Acevedo put his opponent into a joint-breaking thumb lock and slammed him hard, face first, into the row of lockers. Thurmond's face hit the metal so hard it rang as a torrent of blood burst from his nose. Acevedo backed him off a couple of feet and slammed his face into the lockers again, harder this time.

"Whoa there, Chuy," said one of the men watching. "He was just kidding around."

"Anyone else up for a little kidding?" Acevedo asked, letting Thurmond drop to the floor as he looked at the spectators.

The next day he'd duct taped a box of tampons to the front of Thurmond's locker, to the huge amusement of the other officers. Being a cop was not all that different from being an inmate, Chuy reflected. Let a bigger guy fuck you once, and you'd get yourself marked down as a bitch for the duration.

He wondered if they were trying to humiliate him into early retirement. It could be, the way the new chief kept importing cops. Jen Lessing, his new partner, was merely the latest of the imports. From Boston, no less. But Chuy Acevedo remembered when Hispanic cops couldn't get promoted beyond traffic, even here in El Paso, even with a Mexican-American mayor. But he'd survived that era OK, just like he'd survive this one. All the same, cops were enough to make you lose faith in your own mother, not to mention the rest of humanity.

]✳[

Santos lay propped up on pillows, contemplating his discovery, memorizing the body of the young man who lay beside him, lean and taut, angular, all cables and ropes. The gentle rise and fall of his chest, the sloping hill of his hip, the warm and redolent odor of his still excited sex. This male machinery, in its particular proportions and sizes, struck dead center on some lost and long silent chord. And Santos felt it fill his heart like the pealing of a high campanile, the notes rolling like summer thunder over tile roofs, calling long across empty valleys. Look for raunch, find love. Inexplicable world.

Through the window he could see the hillside as it rose behind the house, sketched by silver-white moonlight into a thousand grays punctuated by black, scattered with brightly ascending clusters of rock and dark, clotted thickets of ocotillo. Somewhere near the crest of the hill, kept awake by the brilliance of the moon, a pair of mockingbirds scolded from the candlewoods. He glanced at the clock, surprised by the late hour. He punched down his pillow and rolled toward Tony in the half light. They'd been inseparable for the past two weeks. Long enough for routines to begin to emerge. Santos found himself at ease with the arrangement, even hoping that something more permanent would develop.

"*Qué haces?*" Tony asked.

"Just thinking."

"Thinking?" Tony's eyes calmly studied the shadows of Santos's face. "Serious things?"

"Night things. What do you think about? At night?"

"You really want to know?"

"Sure," Santos said.

"*De veras?*"

"*Sí, de veras.*"

"I think about my father sometimes," Tony replied. "He left my mother, my sisters, and me when I was 7."

Santos slowly traced a line on the boy's skin from the point of the shoulder to the nipple, alert for the shy emergence of some dark knowledge. "Why?" he asked.

"Because of me." Tony rolled onto his back, his face obscured by shadow. "Because he knew already his son was a *joto*. A queer."

Santos pulled the wrinkled sheet up protectively over his lover's chest. "How could he know that? I mean, if you were only 7?"

"Everyone did. Even his friends knew. The whole family knew. Everyone knew about me before I did. When he would take me places with him he would drink too much. When he got drunk he'd get angry for no reason. He would hit me sometimes and say things I didn't understand. So would my uncles and cousins. And when he and my mother weren't around they would make me do things with them. Suck them off. One of my uncles—he was about 17 then—he was the first guy to fuck me. I was maybe 10 or 11 then, I don't remember for sure. But from then on he did it to me every time he could get me alone."

Santos jerked upright in bed, suddenly unable to breathe.

"You OK?" Tony asked.

"Yeah, yeah. You're just...yeah, I'll be OK." Santos inhaled slowly and deeply a couple of times and felt better. His reaction had surprised even him. He hadn't realized how protective of Tony he'd become. "So did you ever see him again, your father?"

"A few times. He started a new family with another woman. Sometimes on the weekends he would come and pick us up, my sister and me. But lots of times he never showed up. I used to wait outside on the steps all day, till after dark, hoping he'd come for us. But not my sister. She knew he wasn't coming. She would go and play with the other kids. After a while he stopped coming completely. After I turned 12 I never saw him again."

"So how did you get to Juárez?" Santos asked.

"My mother moved to Mazatlán. To work to support us. I went to *secundaria* there, but it was hard. After four years I moved to Juárez because I heard they're more tolerant, the people on the border. Back there my mother's brothers told her she should put me in a *prostíbulo*, a whorehouse. Because I was a *puto*."

"*Y tuviste entonces no mas que...cuántos?*"

"I'm not sure. Maybe 14. More or less. When I ran away. *Pues, son cosas de la vida.*"

The things of life: Santos had heard his countrymen saying it for as long as he could remember.

"*Los derechos,*" the boy said, using the word that meant both *straights* and *rights*, "you are nothing to them. In their world you're not even a real person. You get less consideration than an animal. You have no right to exist." He rolled back toward Santos, and Santos wrapped him in his arms. "I'm sick of them. I don't want to live around them anymore. Only with you."

"And your mother?" Santos asked. "What happened to her?"

"She married another man. He already had children. His first wife died, so he had no one to help him. He gets very angry when I go to see her. So she told me it was best if I didn't come there again. She cried. But that was that."

Santos rolled onto his back and pulled Tony on top of him. Santos kissed his eyes and mouth. "I want you to live with me. Only you. Always." And this was not just a thought, or even a whisper. Without calculation, in full affirmation and acceptance of the world's only perfect gift, Santos had finally spoken it out loud.

They lay together for a long time, long after the mockingbirds finished their quarrel and slept, their fingers silently retracing each other in detail, engraving one another in time.

The way Tony took Santos urgently inside himself for the second time that night, avidly pushing himself onto the thickness of Santos's sex, brought their lovemaking to the brink of violence. Santos collapsed on him afterward, encircled his chest with his arms, and inhaled the clean, animal scent of his hair. "I love you," he said.

"*Yo te amo también. Y mucho,*" Tony answered, turning in the dark to kiss him.

| * |

Two days later, Gregorio called to give Santos his next assignment, an order that had come down through the byzantine labyrinth of connections that insulated the new bosses from the old mistakes. Things were different now that the new bosses had come in. The new *jefes* were all business, cooler. The old bosses had been *montañeros, remediados a medias,* cocaine cowboys from the high country of Sonora and Sinaloa, unsophisticated *nuevos ricos* for whom discretion was a sure sign of cowardice.

No one really knew who the new leaders were. They were reputed to be international terrorists, high ranking military, the uppermost echelons of the Federal Judicial Police, senators ousted during the last elections, ex-presidents, any or all of the above. There were many rumors, which in the Mexican tabloids passed for facts. The traditional secrecy of the nation's political and judicial process only added to the press paranoia. One thing, however, remained beyond doubt: The new cartel's secrecy and reputation for retribution gave the police few fingerholds and even fewer surviving witnesses. That morning's phone call from Gregorio, Santos knew, would ratchet up the conflict a great many notches.

CHAPTER THREE

Neal Pearson slammed his elbow into the bag, rotating his entire torso from the hip, just the way J.T. had taught him. Each punch and kick had to originate in the body's center of gravity, a hand's breadth below the navel. Just like a batter's swing unwinds from the hips, and not just the shoulders, punches and kicks had to unwind from the site of the mystical *chi* to deliver all the force of which the body is capable.

The 70-pound bag was secured with a taut length of bungee cord that ran from the bottom of the bag to an eye-bolt cemented into the basement floor. That way, instead of merely swinging back when hit, the bag rebounded sharply. The idea, J.T. had patiently explained, was to hit the bag hard a second time as it snapped back. It sharpened the reflexes. First body-slam your opponent into something solid, then follow up with a lightening fast elbow shot to the windpipe when the guy rebounded back. Neal figured J.T. would know if anyone would. J.T. was a cop, and he'd assured them he'd used the technique many times on the porch monkeys and Mexicans he'd fucked over. "Then you book them for resisting arrest," he'd said, laughing.

To add more realism to the exercise, Lyle and J.T. had

stenciled heads and upper bodies on the sides of the bag, using the same life-sized stencils they painted on the targets at the group's hidden shooting range. The target nigger's head sported an oversized afro, but you didn't get points for the hair. You had to hit him in the face. While J.T. spray-painted the face on the bag, he'd told them niggers were proof the Indians fucked buffalos. Neal still laughed every time he thought of that. By far the best nigger joke he'd ever heard.

Neal practiced some more elbow shots and then switched to heel-palms, concentrating hard on shooting the blow through the face. J.T. had taught them that hitting at the surface of a target would waste most of the power of the punch. The goal was to hit six inches beyond the surface, to shoot through it. The heavy bag snapped back and forth from the blows, and Neal timed his elbow shots to coincide with each backlash, catching the target neatly across the throat. When an object moving in one direction collided with an object moving in the opposite direction, the momentum of each contributed to the total force of the impact, like two cars hitting each other head on. "Hit your man while he's still moving toward you," J.T. had explained. "It adds the force of his momentum to the impact of your elbow. Just some basic physics." Neal had never actually taken physics, but he got the idea.

Neal wished Lyle could have made it. Lyle always went after the bag with a fury, as if he could see and smell the real person the bag represented. J.T. was always commending Lyle. Said he kept focused. Focused was one of the best things you could be in J.T.'s book. Besides, Neal knew he could always work out longer and harder if Lyle was around. When he worked out alone, like tonight, he got tired a lot quicker.

For the next 15 minutes Neal diligently slammed home heel-palms in rapid succession, right, left, right, left, right, left, then...*bam!* A sudden elbow to the throat. Sometimes he surprised his opponent with a knee socked up hard into the guy's balls. Neal wondered what it would feel like, to really hit a guy there. Pretty super, he guessed. Thinking about it made him feel strangely excited somehow, almost elated.

Finally he stopped, exhausted. Sweating and breathing heavily, he clung to the bag and looked around the basement. On the far wall hung the red and black banner with the Creed:

PURE BLOOD

PURE SPIRIT

PURE NATION

Neal guessed Lyle wasn't going to show, so he decided to call it a night. He pulled a gray sweatshirt over his lanky frame, gathered his gear and his towel, turned off the basement light, and headed up the wooden stairs into the main auditorium of the church.

CHAPTER FOUR

D

ígame!"

"I'm in the far right lane. My parking lights are on."

"*Excelente*...OK, I see you. Pull ahead of us and we will follow you. You have the map, *por si acaso?*"

"*Sí. Todo está en orden?*" Santos kept his voice casual and hoped the mandatory frisking he'd receive when they arrived at the compound would be done as a simple matter of course like the last time. If not, he'd definitely be staying in Mexico more and enjoying it less.

"*Sí,*" his contact replied. "*Todo listo. No hay pedo, amigo.* Our man's there. You're headed right for him. *No hay problema.*"

"*Muy bien.*" Santos tossed the flip phone on the seat, and edged the vehicle forward into the narrow lane of the inspection checkpoint. As he pulled up to the window, the uniform snapped his right hand up in a half salute and waved him into Mexico unimpeded. The battleship-gray Rover waiting ahead flashed its lights once as he passed and pulled in behind him. He doused his parking lights. Nothing from here on should attract attention to the vehicle.

He followed the Malecón out to Lopez-Mateos, hung a tight right, followed the wide street down to Triunfo de la República, and turned left, still shadowed by the gray Rover.

For the next 20 minutes he drove, past the malls and high-rise hotels, then past the airport, to the edge of the city, careful to maintain a legal speed. Even if he were pulled over for a traffic violation, real or invented, there would be no problem. The simple mention of his destination would guarantee that. But why take unnecessary chances?

On the outskirts of Juárez they swung off the main highway onto a secondary road, and from that into a long driveway that snaked its way between tall overhanging trees to a high steel gate. Mobile cameras in continuous operation were mounted on the walls above the gate. One emitted a thin, metallic purr as its lens zoomed in to read Santos's license plate. After a moment, the gates slid silently open and the small convoy entered. This occasion would mark the second time that Santos had been summoned here.

Santos's first visit to the compound, the year before, had impressed him like no other meeting before or since. The families of the cartel functioned like an enormous power grid that connected members of government, the police, the army, and who knew who else north of the border.

"Santos! How are you, my friend?" Gregorio thrust out a dry, fleshy hand and Santos shook it. "Back this way." Gregorio jabbed his head toward the back of the hacienda. "You're expected." The two men from the Rover shouldered the five hefty cases Santos had brought across the border, and the group followed Gregorio across the spacious courtyard. "Any trouble with the order?" Gregorio asked. The group had stopped momentarily in a hallway. A tall, muscular man who looked like he took his job very seriously approached Santos and patted him down quickly and expertly, finding nothing. Santos began to breathe again.

"There's always trouble with the order," Santos said, smiling. "That's why you hire me."

Gregorio tossed his oversized head back and barked a short laugh. "You're one smart Mexican…Italian, hell, whatever, motherfucker. You always have the answer. And in this business, that's all that counts, *mi amigo*."

Don Carlos, a slender, dapper man, already nodding his approval, rose from his chair as the group entered the enormous dining room. He advanced, still nodding slightly, braced by thick-necked bodyguards. Each of his bodyguards carried a machine pistol, cradled lovingly on the arm.

Next to daughters, guns were the closest things most Mexican men had to real pets.

"Don Carlos." Coming from Gregorio it sounded very official, like announcing, "His Holiness, the Pope." And Santos supposed this gray-haired dandy probably had more power than the pope.

He almost certainly had more money.

"So you are our armorer," the thin man said, directing himself without preamble to Santos.

"Yes, Don Carlos, I have that honor." Santos took the proffered hand, surprised at its smoothness. The older man smiled, not directly at Santos it seemed, but at something only he appeared to see. Assuming everything was working, the tiny video lens and microphone concealed in Santos's belt buckle had just recorded this priceless exchange.

"Well, let us see what gifts you bring us." Don Carlos made a sweeping gesture to the long wooden table in the middle of the room. It had been previously cleared in preparation for this moment. The two men from the Rover hastened to lay out Santos's wares as *el patrón* and his entourage arrayed themselves along the length of luminously polished cedar. "José," the older man said, directing himself to one of the monster bodyguards, "have the servants bring our friend something to drink."

"*Con permiso,*" Santos murmured, making his way around the table to face the press of expectant faces.

Santos accepted three fingers of Chivas on the rocks, placed his glass on a coaster to protect the finish, and ignored the drink. Only idiots drank while working. He snapped open the first of five briefcases and lifted out a matte black thumb-hole stock. Next he delivered the barrel and receiver, swiftly assembling the takedown rifle with a short series of muted clicks. He attached the bulky scope to the rail and held the reconstructed firearm out to his host. The older man took it in his hands, hefted it and shouldered it smoothly. The old guy was no stranger to longarms.

"It is very light," Don Carlos remarked. "Superb balance."

"Only four and one-half kilos with optics," Santos replied. "The balance, as you noted, is perfect. The stock is fiberglass, the very latest McMillan bolt action suitcase rifle, legally available only to government agencies. This is the latest model to be acquired by United States Secret Service sharp-shooters for executive protection. If you would please sight on something distant, you will see the most remarkable feature of this particular weapon."

Don Carlos complied, sighting through the window to the fountain on the far side of the courtyard. "*Increíble...totalmente increíble,*" he murmured. "It works like an automatic camera lens!"

"*Sí, patrón,*" Santos replied, smiling at his patron's reaction. "Very much. This is actually a prototype, a smart scope. It contains sensors that adjust the optics for any distortion caused by temperature. It also senses wind velocity and direction and adjusts to correct the trajectory. It has a built in laser range finder accurate to within a few centimeters out to a range of 1,500 meters. Also an integral Simrad night sight automatically activated by conditions of low light. The range finder adjusts automatically for trajectory decay. All the shooter does is acquire the target, wait for the green dot in the upper right corner of the field to flash, and squeeze the trigger."

The members of the group exchanged looks. A few raised their eyebrows at one another. Some pressed forward for a closer look.

"Amazing technology." Don Carlos turned the longarm over lovingly in his hands, admiring its details. "The lengths we go to in order to kill each other, eh?"

The men in the group chuckled, as if on cue.

"It has accessories," Santos said. "Two Harris bipods, which open to different heights." He extracted one of the bipods, and laid it in the lid of the open case. "And, of course, a suppressor." He removed a slender, 14 inch tube from the case and held it up in front of the group. The tube's matte black finish exactly matched that of the rifle. "This particular item must obviously be used only with subsonic rounds. But it is excellent for ranges less than 300 meters. It is a customized special manufacture for this particular rifle. Very effective. Barely audible more than a couple of meters away." Santos reached into the open crate. "This," he said as he held it up for the group to see, "is a .308 caliber round manufactured especially for sniping. A third generation super-slick, with the ballistic tip familiar to hunters. These rounds, however, suffer little or no deflection as they pass through glass. The Israelis have found them very useful for hunting terrorists." He held up one of the bullets with its characteristic stretched ogive tip. "The green band indicates it's subsonic."

The group leaned in over the remaining cases and examined the five matching sets of rifles with unconcealed interest, the murmur of their badinage punctuated at intervals with bursts of laughter and exclamations of admiration. Santos stood apart, pretending to sip his Chivas and watching.

Someone took him gently by the arm. Turning, his eyes met the cool gaze of Don Carlos.

"I am very impressed, Mr. De La O. You exceed your already excellent reputation. To where does your expertise extend, if I may ask?"

"To wherever it may be needed, *patrón*." Santos felt an insistent cramp in his pelvis. The camera body wanted out, but this was hardly the time or place.

"We will call on you soon, no doubt. My men will accompany you back across the border now. You will please follow them."

"*Para servirle, patrón. Es un gran placer conocerle.*" Santos said, bowing his head slightly as custom demanded.

"*Igualmente,*" Don Carlos replied. He smiled his enigmatic smile as he turned to speak to someone else. As Santos left the room, the older man motioned for Gregorio to approach.

"*Sí, patrón?*" the fat man inquired.

"He did well," the boss remarked. "Very well indeed."

"*Sí, patrón. El jovenazo tiene mucho talento.*" Gregorio waited expectantly for his boss to direct the conversation.

"Could he get something...more advanced, do you think?" The older man now faced Gregorio directly for the first time.

"I'm sure of it," Gregorio answered. "He's very resourceful. With lots of contacts."

"Very well." The boss nodded, clearly pleased. "Keep close tabs on him. His services will prove convenient later. *Entendido?*"

"*Sí, patrón,*" the fat man answered, nodding. He opened his mouth to ask something, but Don Carlos had already turned and begun to talk to another of his men.

It took some effort for Santos to pick out the spotter at the top of the bridge, a skinny kid this time, a boy hawking lacy tablecloths to the mostly indifferent motorists. As the boy walked back and forth between the lanes of traffic, he watched the uniformed Border Patrol agents who changed checkpoints randomly on the half hour. As Santos's SUV crawled toward the inspection point, the kid approached and directed him into the correct lane. Santos pulled up to the checkpoint, noting the officer's alert Mexican features, relieved not to have encountered another flat Anglo face ruddy with principles. After a cursory examination of his vehicle, the agent waved him through. Santos sighed, some of the tension draining from him. Right that minute, though, he would have traded everything he'd made on the deal for 10 minutes alone in a toilet.

| * |

Santos stretched out in the sparsely furnished living room and savored a Black Russian, the package he'd brought back from Don Carlos's hacienda open at his side. He extracted four of the new hundreds at random from the bundles in the package and held them up to the light, examining the watermarks and security strips. The bills were genuine. He set aside two of the bundles, and tossed the others back into the pile. At length he arose, walked into the bedroom, and stacked the rest of the money in the wall safe. He'd often wondered how it would feel to arrive at this point. How it would be to break out of the small deals, the scut work, and really connect. Not just to be comfortably situated, but really there, moving first-class stuff. The rifles with their miraculous scopes had run to over 100 big. His commission had amounted to 50% of the total order. He let the satisfaction wash over him, as warm and clear and full of the moment as sunlit waves that gently expire on some tropical beach.

The minute he'd gotten home, he'd removed the sleek metallic cylinder that housed the camera body, using gentle traction on the wiring. His ass would be sore for a couple of days. Although the housing had been designed to evade everything but cavity searches, it was not all that small. The belt with the fancy cowboy buckle, concealing the camera's lens, had been stowed in the closet. Santos hated shit-kicker belts but had worn this one to his last several meetings with Gregorio, *sans* wire, letting his boss grow accustomed to its presence. Any unfamiliar item of clothing might have been noticed and aroused suspicion, a risk Santos could not afford to take. The film from the meeting would be stored in a safe deposit box in case someone tossed his house. At the first opportunity, the bulk of his money would be moved to an anonymous offshore account.

Had he been stupid or smart to record the exchange? Stupid, of course, from the standpoint of the cartel. People had been killed for even contemplating less of a betrayal. But smart if he ever needed some measure of protection from the law, something to trade for immunity or a lighter sentence. Might it be possible to blackmail the cartel with the tape? Buy his freedom? He doubted the cartel would ever submit to such humiliation. But who, besides Don Carlos and Gregorio, might be on that tape, his image caught in passing? With computer enhancement, a law enforcement agency might produce miracles from that tiny spool.

]✳[

"Between you and me, I have no problem with it. You like your boys? Big fuckin' deal. So did half the geniuses from the Cinquecento, you know. The very best of them, a bunch of butt-fucking culattini, *if you'll pardon the expression, but that's what they were. But..."* his uncle Vito the Fixer paused, *"they gave us most of the greatest art in Firenze,* capisci? *If it*

was up to me, naturally I'd use you. You know that. You and me, we've always been like this." Vito held up crossed fingers. *"But I can't employ no* finocchio *in this business, if you'll pardon the expression. I don't mean nothing personal, Santos. But you know this is true. The bosses are still very old-country. If it gets back to them that you fuck guys, you're as good as dead here. Even your father, who has always been, just between you and me, a* cafone...excuse *me for saying this about my own brother. He's never had half your style. And you're way smarter than he is. Hell, if you want to know something, you're smarter than most of these guys. But that's not the point."* As if Vito had really insulted his brother, Santos's father, whose favorite saying, "Sono il figlio piú cafone di genitori cafoni," Santos had heard on a regular basis for at least 20 years—his father's way of reminding his son that his very existence was the result of his old man's sexual slumming. Santos, bastard son of his father's Mexican mistress.

"Well, I appreciate you saying that," Santos said. *"I mean, I know that's the case, that things wouldn't work out here. Besides, I couldn't put you in a position like that with the family."*

"Yeah, that's right. Well, no, not really right, but that's the way it is. I can't override these guys. That's just how it is." Vito shrugged. *"Anyway, here's what I want you to do. You take this."* His uncle pushed a fat bundle across the desk. *"It's 100 grand. And I can make you some connections."*

"No, no, no. Come on. I can't take your money like that."

"No, you fuckin' come on. That's nothin' compared to what you'd make if you stayed here and worked in the business. Fuck that. I'll make that back in a week, two at most. You take this and start yourself a business. You're smart. It'll fly. And you keep in touch. You ever need something, I'm

here." Uncle Vito held out the package of bills containing his queer nephew's future.

"*And don't take what I said about* culattini *and stuff personally, OK? You prefer gay, fine. Gay it is. It's just the way I talk, the way I was raised. Me, personally, I eat snatch, the blacker the pussy, the better. I guess to some people, that's disgusting. Fuck them anyway. What do I care what they fuckin' think? They can kiss my fat wop ass. It's just that I can't bring no* fica nera *into the family,* capisci? *Some of the old bosses still believe the only soul black people have is in their music.*" Vito pressed the money into Santos's hands.

| ⋆ |

That had been three years ago. Santos had started his own business, and Uncle Vito had been right. It had not only flown, it had soared.

Santos and Tony were passing over Vegas even now. From the window of the plane, Tony watched the deserts and mountains unfold below them. Santos pretended to doze. They'd be landing at SFO soon, taking the shuttle to a bed and breakfast in the Castro, hitting Santos's favorite sites. And while they were here decompressing, Santos knew he would have to make some decisions about the future. His and Tony's future.

CHAPTER FIVE

Daniel Sexton tucked several well-worn manila folders into his briefcase, turned off his reading light, and locked the door to his office before leaving the empty building. Riding the elevator down to the executive parking area, he reflected on the work remaining. The agency was clearly in trouble. No doubt about it. The director had a hearing before the appropriations committee in only two more weeks, and patience in Congress had been wearing thin lately. He could feel their support eroding, washing away like so much sand. He tossed the briefcase into the back seat of the sedan and started to turn on the radio but changed his mind. Lately music just annoyed him, and he sure as hell didn't need to hear any more goddamn talk. He needed to think this thing out and a silent commute to Georgetown might be just the thing.

News of officials on the take had leaked out again, had all the liberal muckraking magazines scratching at the door. The scent of corruption hung over the agency, tainting every victory. The director had refused to be interviewed by the hyenas at *60 Minutes*, a fact the show had been at pains to report in their typically smug, insinuating manner. But what else could the agency do? After all, the networks insisted on complete control over content and editing so they could sensationalize everything, select juicy sound bites, and scramble things to suit themselves. Ratings. That was all it came down to. Audience and market shares. God, Sexton hated the media. The bastards.

He whipped the car out of the garage, driving too fast. He checked himself, told himself to calm down, slow down, and forget about the media whores. Things could be worse. At least he wasn't in charge of operations in Colombia. Three advisors down in flames in a chopper. Three more men than the country had lost in the entire Kosovo operation, as the editorials had been quick to point out.

Sexton noted his reflection in the rear-view mirror. He looked pale, drawn, older. He needed some sun. He'd be glad when they finally wrapped up this damned operation. Their principle contact in Sinaloa had broken off. The local agents feared the worst, but, as usual, they couldn't confirm. Sexton's boys never knew who played on what team in that god-forsaken sewer of a country.

Things in the field hadn't changed much, even with the new administration in place. Trust was out of the question. They'd been screwed over again and again. Nothing would ever really be done about the corruption. It was ubiquitous, everlasting, and everybody knew it. Merely mention it, and all you heard about was the precious trade with Mexico, the balance of payments, goodwill, national sovereignty, good neighbors, respect for their efforts, the men and money it had cost them, always another goddamn excuse not to stamp out corruption on the Mexican side.

Hell, Sexton thought, we might just as well invade the goddamn place. Annex it. Half their people were already living in the U.S. as it was. The whole subject just made him sick. Fuck their goddamn sensibilities. Everybody down there pretending to relive the whole Mexican-American War while they bribed and stole and murdered. They'd want to renegotiate the goddamn Treaty of Guadalupe Hidalgo next. When, he wondered, would the U.S. government stop letting the Mexicans string them along? Stop bending over for this crap? It made him furious.

How had he gotten into this, anyway? It was like sinking in quicksand. He was more of a politician now than a law enforcement officer, and that wasn't the way he'd planned things. He'd really screwed up somehow but couldn't put his finger on where. And now they were going to find their Sinaloan contact in a shallow grave on some *narcotraficante's* ranch. He could just feel it. "God-fucking-damn them," he cursed to himself.

Sexton's mind was still racing when he pulled into the driveway. He just wanted to get the hell inside, get a drink. He wondered if he'd been drinking too much lately. Given what they put him through at the agency, that would be easy enough to do. Slip into it unaware, his mind on something else. At any rate, that's what dear Martha maintained. Hammered on nonstop, in fact. His mind always somewhere else. He dragged his work home with him, reading long after she'd given up on sex and fallen asleep. Pulling that job around like a ball and chain. He'd turned into Marley's ghost. Her description of him: Marley's ghost. In the last year Martha had turned into a real ball-busting bitch.

Now he couldn't find the remote to the garage door. Damn it all to hell. That was the kind of day it had been. He ran his right hand over the surface of the passenger seat. Still couldn't locate the goddamned thing. Shit. He turned on the dome light, started to grope around under the seats. Damn it, there it was. On the dashboard all this time. Right in front of him. "I must be fucking losing it," he spat.

The bullet punched a clean, round hole through the side

window glass and hit Sexton just over the left ear, its impact snapping his head forward as his brains sprayed onto the windshield. A dark stain spread over his pants as his bladder emptied. His body sagged leisurely downward, its muscle tone already dissipating in random quivers and tics as his dead foot slipped off the brake pedal. The car coasted slowly backward into the street and came to rest with a crunch against a neighbor's Mercedes. The impact triggered the luxury car's alarm, which shrilled into the darkened street as Daniel Sexton slid face-down onto the floorboard, knees bent beneath him and head sagging forward, his posture a grotesque parody of prayer.

Behind a hedge more than 100 meters up Sexton's street, the shooter quickly broke down his weapon and dropped the components into a backpack. He walked calmly from the scene to his car, unable to suppress a wry smile. The rifle had performed every bit as well as he'd been assured it would. This new scope was sorcery itself.

| ✳ |

Neal peered through the back window of the Camaro at the deserted streets, as excited as he'd ever been but trying to play it cool. Ron Schneider sat on the other side of the back seat, a thin wisp of smoke drifting from his nostrils. He cracked the rear window and performed another steady draw on the cigarette, holding it between his ring and middle fingers like he'd seen some guy do in a movie. As Ron smoked, Neal pretended not to study the tattoo on the back of his hand.

"So you like that, huh?" Schneider asked, blowing a thin stream of smoke in Neal's direction.

"Like what?" Neal replied, caught.

"The tattoo, dumb-ass. Bet you don't even know what it is, do ya?"

Neal shrugged nervously and shook his head. No, he didn't know what it was.

"Double lightening bolt, man. Waffen SS. The best, man. Killers. The bitchinest."

"Oh, yeah," was the only thing Neal could think of to say. His response sounded pretty lame even to him.

"Oh, yeah," Schneider repeated, mocking him. "Hey, Lyle," he said to the Camaro's driver. "This little jerk has no fucking idea, man. What the hell are you teachin' these new guys? He don't know shit!"

Neal felt his face burning. He hated how easy it was to make him blush. He hoped it was too dark in the car for Ron to notice.

Ed Farris twisted his bulk around in the passenger's side of the front seat so he faced Schneider. "Well, Ronnie, maybe someday he'll be a big skinny asshole just like you and get his-self a big bad-ass Waffen SS tattoo!"

Ron got under everybody's skin, Neal guessed.

"Well, we'll find out tonight if the little fucker has balls or not, won't we?" Schneider shot back. "One way or another, it's no hair off my ass."

"Hell, you probably don't even got no hair on yer ass." Ed sneered, his belly convulsing with laughter. "The real Waffen SS woulda ate yer ass fer breakfast anyway."

"Why don't you little girls all just shut the fuck up!" Lyle exploded. "I swear to God, you sound just like my goddamn little sisters! Next thing I know, you'll be pulling hair!" Neal suddenly felt much better. Lyle always kept everybody else in line. "We're out here hunting for fags, and you guys are fighting like a bunch of kids!"

"So you say they're coming back down here, huh?" Ron asked.

"Yeah, that's what I'm saying." Lyle replied, still irritated.

Neal knew that Lyle didn't much like guys who smoked. He said it was filthy. That was probably why he and Ron didn't get on so well.

"Hell," Lyle added. "That fag bar on Paisano, the one on San Antonio, another over on Kansas Street, that fucking huge one on Overland. They aren't fucking *coming back*, they never left! The whole damn area's infested with 'em." Lyle slowed and pulled the Camaro onto one of the streets that ran along the plaza. Weeknights there were always fags hanging out there.

"Well, they'll by God start leaving here after tonight," Ed observed, turning back around and getting himself comfortable again in the seat. "We'll run their faggot asses outta here."

"Hey *chula!*" someone on the street shouted. The four men looked in the direction of the voice. "I said, hey bitch!" A young Latino on the Texas Street side of the park was shouting at a tall black man in drag. The black queen just kept on, hips swiveling, and ignored the heckler. He came to a stop at the curb—his right hand perched on his hip—across the street from the park.

"I said, you cock-sucking black-ass *puta* bitch!" the Latino boy shrilled.

"Fuck you and *chinga tu puta madre!*" the black queen shot back, finally annoyed.

"It's about fucking time you talk to me like a living person, Liticia Bitch!"

"What the muthafuck you...JoNell? JoNell, that you? What you doin' dress like that? You go'n crazy, bitch? Shit! I thought you was some *man!*" The two figures approached, embraced. A considerably more subdued conversation began that the men in the car couldn't overhear.

The intensity of the exchange at the edge of the park masked the cautious opening of the Camaro's door and the rough sound it made as it scraped against the concrete curb. The four men unfolded from the car's cramped interior and huddled briefly together beyond the glare of the street lights. "Ed, you and Ron get up ahead of him," Lyle whispered. "Me and Neal, we'll follow him in."

The four men split into pairs and entered the park, their progress marked by the soft scraping of steel-toed boots on pavement.

The conversation at the curb ended. The Latino youth headed away from the park, toward his favorite hangout. Hips provocatively swaying, the tall, stately figure of the drag queen sauntered into the park, toward the center of the plaza, in the direction of the alligator sculpture. Lyle and Neal fell into step behind her, trailing her to her left. Up ahead on the right Ron and Ed waited on a bench, sitting in the shadows. Neal Pearson pulled a telescoping steel whip from the holster on his belt at the same time that Lyle drew one from under his jacket. Lyle nodded to Neal in the darkness. With a flick of the wrist, each whip extended with a sinister metallic *zi-i-ing*.

Startled by the noise, their target spun around. Neal moved forward and swung the whip with his full force, smashing it into the drag queen's throat just as her head came around. Neal felt the steel bite into the flesh and heard the moist crunch as the gristle of the windpipe shattered. A high-pitched whining sound emanated from a gash in the target's neck as she tried to suck air in through her shattered trachea. She staggered a couple of steps and fell soundlessly to her knees, unable to breathe, Lyle's steel-toed boot shearing into her ribs as she went down. Neal heard the soft wet explosion from the drag queen's neck as the force of the kick drove the remaining air from her chest. She rolled to her side, her blond wig at a ridiculous angle, and received a kick in the face from Ron. Suffocating, she struggled upward, her front teeth hanging by threads, and lunged forward, gulping frantically for air. Neal stepped in and hit her hard with the whip, opening up her face. The target fell to her elbows. Neal followed up with another kick to the chest. A small gurgle of bubbles escaped from her open throat and floated downward in a stream of blood from her flayed cheek and nose. The four attackers closed in on her wordlessly, raining kicks into her writhing form.

Back in the car, Neal laughed in short, silly bursts, still jittery from the adrenaline. This had been his first ever boot party.

"Look at him, guys. He's wound up tighter'n a two-dollar watch! You did good, man. Real good." Ron lit a Winston and shot Neal a real smile and a fake punch in the arm. "That there's some wild shit, huh? You were digging that, huh?"

Neal grinned back, feeling better than he ever had. Like a man. Like one of the guys.

In the front seat, Lyle checked his watch. They'd been in the park seven short minutes.

"Cured that nigger faggot," Ed observed.

Lyle cranked the Camaro and pulled back from the curb, making the tires squeal, and headed toward the interstate. "Who's in the mood for a beer?" he asked.

In the back seat, Ron and Neal laughed and high-fived each other.

In the street behind the park, a pair of headlights came on. A black-and-white patrol car pulled slowly away from the curb and made a leisurely pass by the park before turning in the direction of the police station.

]★[

Jenna Lessing flipped on the coffee maker, yawned and stretched, and stared balefully at the glowing red numerals on its face. Fred had been gone two hours already. He had six surgeries on the schedule this morning. Which was good. They could use the money. She pulled her housecoat together against the early morning chill as she went back toward the master bedroom to start the shower. Up here on the mountain the air stayed cooler than down in the valley and Jenna treasured the relative chill. Boston had been hot in the summer. Muggy. But nothing like this. She'd never get used to the heat in El Paso.

She picked up the remote and clicked on CNN, returning to the bathroom to resume her morning ritual. "Shit, shave, and shower," her father had always called it. Even now the smallest things reminded her of him. From the bathroom she overheard the words "DEA" and "apparent assassination." Naked, with her toothbrush and its neatly deposited line of paste in hand, she hurried back into the bedroom, arriving just in time to see Daniel Sexton's face fade from the screen before the announcer moved on to the next item of morning news. What the hell had that been about?

She kept the news on in the kitchen as she sipped her first coffee, but the item didn't repeat. She finished dressing and made the rounds of the house, giving the window locks a last minute check. Her cell phone trilled as she closed the front door.

"Jen?" Her male coworkers had always called her "Jen." Chopped off, monosyllabic, like Ben or Len. Or *men*.

"Good morning, Chuy. What's up?"

"Had breakfast?" Acevedo asked.

"Nope." She untangled her keys as she walked down the driveway. The morning air felt fresh; the western slope of the mountain was still deep in shade at this hour.

"Well, meet me over at the county morgue. Early start. Then I'll take you to breakfast. Rincón. My treat."

"Sounds swell. The breakfast part, not the morgue. Twenty minutes?"

"Yeah. Great. See ya." She dropped the phone into her purse. As she drove down the slope past the upscale homes and schools, her mind drifted back over the disturbing fragments of the news report. So much transport of cocaine, black-tar heroin, and marijuana took place in and around El Paso that the story, whatever its details, would surely impact the local police department in some way. She continued to mull over what she'd heard as she patiently negotiated the morning log-jam on I-10.

CHAPTER SIX

We need to talk. Call me on a land line." Gregorio reeled off a number. Santos dropped the flip phone into the pocket of his sweatpants and slipped out of the pec deck. He used a calling card for the gym's pay phone. Afterward, as he headed back to the Smith machine for more shoulder presses, he stopped to watch as Tony struggled upward from the depths of a hack squat. He'd been going at it valiantly for several months but had failed to gain more than a couple of pounds.

"I've got to see an associate later," Santos said. "Only for an hour, maybe two. How about a pizza afterward?"

"Ardovino's?"

"Sure. Sounds great."

"This isn't going anywhere, is it?" Tony locked the machine down and stepped out, his legs quivering. "I've been busting my ass, and I don't see any difference."

"You don't have the genes, baby. Anyway, look at me. I've been lifting 12, almost 13 years now. But I'm not huge, not like some of these guys. Face it, *manito*, there's no Incredible Hulk in either of us."

"Yeah, easy for you to say. You're no *flacote*. *Mírame, no más*, I'm skinny!"

"Yeah, well, as you should know better than anyone, I dig skinny guys. You make me horny. All the time. I love you the way you are. I think you're perfect." They'd had this conversation so many times already. Each time Tony refused to be reassured. Santos would have liked nothing better than to kiss him right there, a long, deep kiss that tasted of sweat.

Instead, Santos went back to the bench press. He lay on his towel between sets, watching the passing men scrutinize themselves and each other in the mirrored walls, some with satisfaction, others with disappointment. He felt relieved to be away from that part of it, at least for now. Why, he wondered, was the power to attract more intoxicating than the satisfaction of having? Why was falling in love more exhilarating than being in love? Why all this hunger, this urge to live in a state of constant frisson?

As he resumed his bench press, driving the bar upward, again and again, the cords of his chest straining against his skin, it came to him, what he must do now. A revelation without trumpets. Some guys stayed with the business until they were death-struck. But not him. He would be ready to quit soon, to take his money, take his lover, and go. To walk on the beach on Cozumel, Tony at his side, as the sun rose through misty sea clouds. To sit on a patio in San Miguel de Allende, a breeze rustling in the purple and red bougainvillea. To stand on a hill overlooking Florence, his arm around Tony, the duomo below, its majestic dome silver in the moonlight. There would be so many things to do, moments to share. Before he ended up in prison or dead. Because sooner or later every player's luck ran out. Most of them didn't believe it or just didn't care. But Santos believed, and since he and Tony had become lovers, Santos cared.

] ✫ [

"I'm telling you, *mano*, they're going to war. No more fucking around." Gregorio stirred his rice and beans together, then dumped generous portions of green salsa on top of the concoction. "They want something very sophisticated, OK? Not that charity shit like the *pinche* CIA gave those crazy sand niggers so they could shoot down Russians!" Filet mignon with beans and rice. The man's taste in food and the quantity he consumed never failed to amaze.

"That's going to be very tough to get, to say nothing of expensive. Something that accurate. Small enough to carry around like that and still have a workable range." Santos took a bite of steak. Since Sexton's death, the U.S. had stepped up its interdictions and applied much more pressure than usual on the Mexican government to crush the cartel. But apparently the Americans weren't the only ones determined to play hardball.

"I told them if anyone could put this thing together, you could. I put my head on the block for you, *compa*."

This fat-ass sack of grease wouldn't stick his neck out for his own mother, Santos thought. Gregorio knew perfectly well he could get this. He'd definitely have to work his connections, but he could get it.

"They just don't want to have to fuck around with a complex system," Gregorio reiterated. "They want to keep it simple enough to turn over to just about any competent guy out in the field." The fat man glanced around at the other diners, keeping his voice low. "So they don't have to train a bunch of guys for months on how to use the things."

Great, Santos thought. That meant the cartel planned on striking back soon, and hard.

"They were very impressed with the rifles, by the way," Gregorio added, between bites.

Santos's eyes wandered to the head of a moose mounted

on the restaurant's front wall. The moose hadn't put *its* head on the block, but here it was, nonetheless, hanging on the wall of a Mexican restaurant, its glass eyes watching humans eat. Life had a way of taking weird turns like that.

Daniel Sexton had been the third ranking man at the DEA, with direct oversight of Mexican and Central American ops. He was the highest ranking member the agency had ever lost and a much higher ranking man than they'd ever expected to lose. According to what Santos had read, the killing remained unsolved. Mexico had lost two upper-echelon members of their attorney general's staff—probably both of the honest ones. And Mexico had no arrests or suspects either—at least none that had been made public. The cartel had made its point. But the Americans, badly entangled in Colombia, wanted a full-court press. As a matter of national pride, Santos assumed. The Americans. Hubba, hubba. Never say die, never wise up.

"*Pero, sabes qué?* I think that was almost like a kind of test, you know? Like they were leading up to this." Gregorio looked at him expectantly.

"I can put this together for you," Santos said without speculating on what the cartel might or might not have been leading up to. "But with one condition. I disappear for a while after this deal. For a year, maybe more." If they didn't want to train men to operate complicated weapons, then they planned to use the damn things sooner rather than later. Which would make next year an excellent time to be on an extended vacation.

"That's possible. They would go for that," Gregorio mumbled through a mouth full of food.

Did the fat man understand? Did he really know what taking down a DEA plane or a military chopper would unleash? Santos watched as Gregorio forked another piece of rare steak into his mouth. All things considered, aside from the fact that he was a natural slimebag, Gregorio was a decent liaison. And he surely knew or at least sensed something about Santos's sexual relationships. Guys like Gregorio didn't stay alive by not knowing the details. Strange, he thought, Mexican men. Hung up about sexuality, but open to desire. As long as things were not specified, pretenses were maintained and real problems were uncommon. After a time, even veiled kidding and sexual innuendo could take place. Within limits. *Un secreto a gritos*, they called it. A shouted secret. But unproblematic so far. And as long as he was perceived as an exclusive top, a macho man, a man's man, *un hombre de a de veras, de pelo en pecho*, things would probably remain that way.

"So what happens if they take down a DEA plane over Mexico?" Santos asked.

Gregorio stopped eating. He appeared to actually be thinking about the consequences. "That would be a real *chingadera*," he said after several moments of reflection. "That would put everybody on the spot. The Mexicans and the Americans."

"Exactly. That would be a major *paso en falso*. A real and true pooch-fuck. So if they do it, better in U.S. airspace, *verdad*?"

"*Cierto*. You don't shit where you eat." Gregorio went back to his steak.

"But," Santos said, "if they take down a plane in U.S. airspace, that's like a declaration of war. The response would be total."

Gregorio actually laid down his fork, his next bite of steak still impaled on it.

"And if they could do that," Santos said, "take out a DEA plane, they could just as easily take down a 747. The Americans will respond accordingly. You know many

CUT TO THE BONE

Americans are not convinced that there's any way to really stop drug traffic. But the U.S. government will label this 'terrorism.' That's a whole different issue. Once they call it terrorism they can do pretty much anything they want and the public will support it."

"*Con una chingada.*" The round face across the table had grown pensive and paled to a shade of pink. Gregorio's capillaries were like litmus paper. A different color for every reaction.

"It's just that you should know this, *amigo.* That's all I'm saying. It's possible the people calling the shots still don't understand the way Americans are thinking about these things and aren't able to predict the consequences. But you know, and I know, that if this happens, the Americans and every other intelligence service in the world will be on this like a hundred flies on hot shit." Santos paused to gauge his liaison's reaction. He clearly had Gregorio's attention. "If this gets traced back to the cartel or if they claim responsibility, we're going to wake up in the middle of a real cluster-fuck."

Gregorio had gone quite completely pale and appeared to have lost his appetite.

"So this is going to cost your people some serious money, *entiendes?* Cash in full at the time of delivery, and then I'm out. One year, maybe longer. And while you're at it, you cover your own ass. Seriously." After a pause, Santos added, "I'll call you in a couple of weeks and let you know how it's going."

Santos rose and left Gregorio to his meal. He'd promised Tony a pizza at Ardovino's. He'd have to hurry if they were going to make it.

] ✳ [

Chuy Acevedo watched his new partner's reaction as the medical examiner pulled the sheet back. What lay beneath would have made any rookie puke. The guy's face had been flayed, and the bones under the skin broken up like gravel. But whatever Jenna Lessing felt inside, she remained impassive. "How did he die?" was all she asked.

"Fractured trachea, broken ribs. Bilateral hemopneumo-thorax. Smothered to death due to a crushed chest, basically." Acevedo watched as the coroner tugged off his wire frame glasses and smeared the dirt on the lenses with the end of his tie. He'd been an anesthesiologist once, years back. Before he'd started chipping his patients' fentanyl. Then he lost a kid on the table, and not just *some* kid, some *hijo de la vecina*, but another doctor's kid, the guy's oldest son. Lost his license next, which was just about unheard of in Texas. Even did a little time. In another state, of course. At some country club excuse for a prison. That's what they did, Chuy knew. Lose the right to practice in one jurisdiction and just pick up somewhere else, hardly missing a beat.

This morning the M.E. looked particularly withered, burned away. Worse than some of the stiffs he carved up. Hungover and old: a shitty combination. Chuy knew his story. Chuy Acevedo knew everybody's story. Chuy knew where the bodies were buried in this town. The majority of them, at any rate.

"He has a lot of other trauma, fractures, brain full of blood. Overkill. But that's not what did him in. He was basically already dead when all the head stuff happened." The M.E. readjusted his smeared lenses.

"Who found the body?" Lessing asked.

"City worker? Some civilian early to catch a bus? I'm sure it's in the police report, detective." It wasn't the M.E.'s problem who the hell had reported it. "I just establish cause of death."

"Looks like a fag," Chuy observed.

"He was dressed in women's clothes," the coroner said.

"So, yeah, I guess that would make him a fag." The old man pulled his glasses off and examined the lenses critically with watery eyes.

"Would you call it a gay-bashing?"

"A what?" The withered man stared at Lessing.

"A hate crime. Do you read this as a robbery gone bad or as a hate crime?" She looked like she might bite the old man's head off.

This was the first time Acevedo had seen his partner edgy. Chuy felt himself warming toward her.

"Well, whoever it was did this, they weren't exactly secret admirers, were they?" the M.E. said. "Now if you'll excuse me, the Border Patrol's just fished another floater out of the river. Drowned in quicksand, likely as not. They never catch on, Mexicans." The M.E. tossed a sidelong glance at Chuy. "All this and it's not even 9 o'clock yet," he said, turning to walk away. At least his patients didn't call him in the middle of the night whining about their fever and snot, he reflected.

The two detectives found a paltry amount of cash and a cheap watch when they inventoried the belongings. Chuy commented that convenience-store clerks had been murdered for less. Maybe, he suggested, whoever had done it had panicked, or maybe the homo had resisted. But he could tell Lessing wasn't buying any of it. For some reason, the case seemed to get under her skin. Was it just because the guy had been torn up so badly?

They rode in silence to Rincón, Chuy driving. Lessing stared blankly out the window at the university campus as the car wound around Sun Bowl Drive. Acevedo decided to try and lighten up the mood a little. "So, Jen, you know what has six balls and fucks you twice a week?"

"No Chuy, I don't know. What has six balls and fucks you twice a week?"

"The Texas lottery." Chuy turned in time to catch the slight backward toss of the head, her only concession to mirth. He wondered how she behaved away from the job. At work she came across as tight-assed, every loose edge nailed down—that's *Ms.* Robocop to you, jerkwad. Maybe it was because she was new. Being on unfamiliar ground could do that to a person.

"I gotta tell Fred that one," she said. "He'll love it."

An offer of friendship? Chuy wondered. At this rate they might actually become partners some day. What Chuy couldn't figure out, though, was why a doctor's wife would want to be a cop. What was *that* about?

CHAPTER SEVEN

R ain had fallen steadily for the past two days, unusual for San Antonio, and the rental Ford's wipers batted drizzle with a monotonous whomp-whomp, whomp-whomp. Santos rechecked the name of the place and pulled into the parking lot. He found a space near the front, and eased the car up to the fake stone siding of the combination restaurant-bar. He opened the attaché case on the seat beside him and removed the short frame Sig Sauer .45. He tucked the pistol into his waistband, arranged his jacket over it, and stepped out of the car into the warm rain.

The long, narrow restaurant adjoined a wider rectangular pool hall with a bar along its far wall. No haute cuisine here, Santos thought, assailed by the smell of rancid cooking oil after the rain-fresh air outside. In the pool room, two military types appeared to be engaged in a leisurely game at the first table. The taller man wore a black leather vest over a gray sleeveless T-shirt. Tattooed barbed wire circled his arms between his neglected delts and his bulging biceps. The man's shorter companion wore a ratty fatigue jacket bulky enough to conceal a small arsenal. They stopped their game and stared openly at Santos as he walked by, hefting their cue sticks like the bad boys in the cheesy martial arts flicks they undoubtedly watched. Santos shrugged. Sophisticated weaponry, he'd long since learned, as often as not showed up in the most unlikely of hands. These days, in this country, a hydrogen bomb in the back of a camper would not have surprised him. Stupid people the world over had smart weapons. The people more than the weapons were the really scary part.

The seller sat at a table in the very back of the restaurant. He'd pulled a cap with no logo down so the bill partially covered his eyes. A faded fatigue jacket covered his spare frame.

"Randall Jenkins?" Santos asked.

The young man flinched, then nodded weakly, startled that Santos knew his real name.

Santos pulled up a chair, placed the black attaché case on the seat beside him, removed a copy of the young man's dossier, and passed it across to him. "Have a look," he said, his voice neutral.

Jenkins swallowed several times as he leafed through it. "You military intelligence?" he asked.

"Randall, if there really were any such animal, you wouldn't be sitting here trying to sell me missiles. Now, would you? You of all people should know that."

Jenkins shoulders sagged with relief.

"My employers only want you to be aware that you're not the only guy around who can work a computer keyboard, nor, for that matter, are you among the best. You've switched some DRMO codes. You've paid some people. Chump change, because that's all you could borrow on what you're making. You just want to be rich and you decided to take advantage of that computer training that's not good enough for the private sector and the military's well-known inability to keep its own secrets. How am I doing so far?" Santos asked.

A small, bitter smile etched itself on Jenkins's lips.

"Which is just fine by us," Santos continued. "Be all you

can be, right? Just as long as you understand you're not the only guy who can get into people's shit." Santos paused long enough for Jenkins's brain to absorb this reality. "Now if your product is genuine, I'm ready to deal. If it's not, this is your opportunity to back out gracefully. No problems, no questions asked. Because...and I promise you this, Randall...if you're trying to peddle us a load of junk, you, your cheese-dick buddies at the pool table, and every other person you know will die. And not from cancer. And not some day. My employer expects to get what he pays for, and he's not some Colorado militiaman stocking up on 20-year-old Cobra parts. Just so we understand each other completely."

Jenkins glanced back at the pictures in the file. Pictures of his wife and kids, all shot through telephoto. Fear flickered in his eyes.

"So before you lay your cock on the block, Randall, I've got to ask you: Are these things real?" Santos spoke casually, smiling. He let the photos do the threatening.

"Yeah," Jenkins mumbled. "They're real." A waitress had risen from the depths with plates for another table. She pretended not to notice them, and disappeared again into the kitchen.

"So tell me about them. How do they work?"

"Well," Jenkins said, his composure slowly returning, "they're surface-to-air. Fire and forget. Lightweight. Small. Fired from the shoulder." Jenkins's eyes moved back again to the photos of his family. "Designed for peace-keeping missions. Only got a range of about three or four miles, but that's all they need, see, 'cause they're fast." Jenkins licked the dryness from his lips and looked around for the waitress. "They'll catch anything. But you got to get close enough to the target."

"How do they track?" Santos asked, careful to keep the interest from his voice.

"They have some new kind of chip. A data cube, I think they're calling it. Like a regular chip, only more three-dimensional. Stores thousands of times more stuff than a conventional flat chip."

The waitress reappeared. Santos flagged her down.

"What'll ya have, boys?"

"Coffee. Black, please." Santos said.

"Bud Light," Jenkins murmured.

Santos waited until she'd gotten out of earshot. "So how does it acquire the target?"

"It reads the aircraft's total avionics signature. Everything. Smart as hell, like a miniature air-traffic computer."

If he thinks air traffic computers are smart, he's behind the times, Santos thought, but let it slide.

"It doesn't get confused, and it microtargets," Jenkins continued. "Follows the signals right back to the cockpit. And it has... How would you say it? Predictive capacity, I guess. It can predict the pilot's moves, like an algorithm sort of. So it's really hard to shake. It took them forever to R and D this thing."

"How many have you got?"

"Six. With launchers." Jenkins stopped talking while the waitress put down their drinks, asked if they needed anything else, and then left

"When can I see them?"

"Well, right now. If you want to. They're right here. I mean, I've....we've got 'em with us."

"I assume you have a safe account where I can transfer funds? And that you have the necessary codes to make an electronic transfer?"

"Yeah, no problem."

"OK, Randall. It looks like you've done your homework. Let's go have a look at your merchandise." Santos laid a five on the table and they stood to go. "Tell your buddies to stay where I can see them."

The six slender crates were stacked under a tarp in the back of Jenkins's van. The shorter of Jenkins's two body-guards pried the top off one with a small crowbar, revealing the missile's sleek contours. Santos removed the directions from inside the crate. Line drawings, accompanied by instructions in English, French, German, Hebrew, and Arabic, detailed the four simple steps required to acquire a target and shoot it down. There were no instructions in Spanish. Could he assume there were no plans for deployment in Latin America? Destinations aside, the weapons easily surpassed the cartel's requirements.

Using the computer in his case, Santos transferred $2.8 million U.S. from the Banco Nacional de México into Jenkins's account at the International Bank of the Cayman Islands. The transfer of funds was confirmed, the boxes were moved from the van to the trunk of Santos's car. "You know, Randall," he said, handing Jenkins a duplicate of his file, "we're not the monsters you take us for. We're a thousand times worse. Don't forget that if some tin badge ever pitches you a witness protection offer. My bosses will snuff all of your relatives and everybody who graduated from high school with you. Nothing personal, you understand. Just good business. Have a nice life, Randall. You've earned it."

Before returning to the rental car, Santos stood in the rain with his hand under his jacket. His fingers stayed around the Sig's grip until Jenkins's van drove away. It would be such a waste to come this far and end up with a bullet in the back. Keep the money *and* the missiles, sell them again: Unless they were complete fools, the idea must have occurred to them.

Back in his hotel garage, Santos parked the Ford next to a Jeepster he'd rented in El Paso and switched the crates, covering them with a sleeping bag. From the window in his room, high above the streets, he looked out at the Riverwalk below him. A gust of wind blew a volley of rain across the deserted sidewalks and the quaint stone bridges that spanned the shallow water. In this place, in another time, showers of confetti from broken *cascarones* had fallen gently on a lover's laughing face, a face now lost to all but memory. Another blast scoured the sidewalk and his heart. That, as they said, was then. This was now. He turned from the window, picked up his single suitcase, and took the elevator to the lobby. He checked out immediately, leaving the rental car keys at the desk with a moderate tip for the clerk, a sum unlikely to be remembered at some later date.

On the edge of town, he stopped at the first gas station on the interstate, peeled off the beard and mustache he'd worn for the past two days, and burned them in the bathroom sink along with his falsified driver's license and insurance papers. He bought an extra large coffee in the station's convenience store before pulling the Jeepster onto the southbound interstate. That night in Laredo he transferred the shipment over to Gregorio and received payment in full. At around 5 o'clock in the morning he stopped in San Angelo, called Tony, and slept fitfully for a few hours in a drab Motel 6. By 8 o'clock he was up, showered, and back on the road. He'd never stopped thinking about what they'd do with the money. The mere thought of it made him laugh out loud as he drove west across The Big Empty for the last time.

| ★ [

"Why don't we get away for a couple of days?" he asked, walking into the kitchen.

Tony looked up expectantly from the dishes. "Like where?" he asked. "Cloudcroft?"

"No, babycakes, a little further out. Pack that butch red and black checkered shirt we got last week. And don't forget your I.D." Tony's bogus American birth certificate, driver's license and passport would pass the closest scrutiny. Done by the best man in northern Mexico, they'd never merit a second look, regardless of Tony's imperfect command of English. "And don't bother to pack a jacket," Santos added as Tony dried his hands and headed eagerly for the bedroom. "We'll buy you a new one when we get where we're going."

CHAPTER EIGHT

They sat right against the glass in the very front corner of the Bagdad Cafe and watched the parade of Castro street life. Santos glanced at his watch. One-thirty in the morning, the end of a long day. Across the table, Tony sat, barely awake, his progress through his sandwich interrupted by frequent micronaps. Seeing Santos watching him, he gave his lover a drowsy, apologetic smile.

Falling asleep like this, Tony's face appeared childlike. Santos could easily imagine the little boy he'd been. Santos had learned not to waste time worrying about what couldn't be changed, but he wished he could have been around to protect Tony from the cruelty of his childhood. To do that, he reflected, he would have had to be the kid's father, or at least an older brother. And then to become his lover? Screwing your own son? Too weird. Besides, what would he have done with the boy's mother? Maybe he could have been an older friend, he decided. After a few moments reflection on this conundrum, he simply gave up.

He watched Tony in the midst of a longer fit of sleep. If they didn't leave for the bed and breakfast soon, he'd end up having to carry him back. How would that look? He supposed stranger things had been seen on Castro Street. They could live here, he thought. He'd caught himself doing an inventory of the area as they'd moved around it. Noticing the gyms, the rental signs, the post office, and the markets. Special notations of the best streets, the nicer apartments, the nifty restaurants, the clubs, and the cool places to go. Of course the weather here was fantastic. In the 50s at night, in the 70s during the day, a wonderful change from the swelter of West Texas. *Nesting,* he thought with a smile. He was looking for a place to build their nest.

"You about ready?" he asked.

Tony awoke with a start. "Yeah," he replied. "Sorry. I keep falling asleep." The boy regarded him with wan smile.

"Well, we had a long day. We may have overdone it a little." Santos stretched and motioned for the waiter to bring the tab. In fact, they'd overdone it a lot. He'd been too anxious to show Tony the parts of the city they'd missed the first time around, too anxious to reconnect. Somehow being here with Tony just magnified the splendor of the city. He lay the ticket on the table with some bills and they walked out into the brisk night air.

"Thanks again for this," Tony said, touching the leather of the new jacket. "It even matches yours. It's romantic, don't you think?" They'd found it at Worn Out West, a denim and leather store in the heart of the gay district. Tony had liked it even before he realized it matched his lover's.

"Yeah, it's romantic. I was hoping they might still have this style." Santos had always loved the way leather conformed to fit a man's frame. They crossed the street and turned west on Castro, walking uphill in the direction of their bed and sleep.

"So what's next?" Tony asked. "Matching rings?"

Tony had tried to keep his tone light, but Santos was not deceived. Santos knew that Tony loved him, but on another level saw him as an immense stroke of good fortune, a sea change in his life, and for that reason all the more suspect. Tony had never had much luck, and so remained wary despite all reassurances. Even this happiness might be snatched away. Tony believed all good things must come to an end. Santos expected all good things to change into other good things.

"Yeah, as a matter of fact." Santos glanced over at the figure by his side as they labored up the hill. Tony was wide awake now, his breath just visible in the coolness of the air. "If you're willing to make the jump."

Tony put his arm around Santos and held him very tight. "You make me very happy," he said. "I've never felt so loved, and so respected." Tony's voice quavered as though it might break if he said more. Santos returned his embrace as the two walked on in silence.

| ✻ |

Tony came out of the bathroom naked, his hair still wet, followed by a cloud of steam. Smiling, he opened the drawer of the bedside table and pulled out something that looked like thin black leather straps. Santos looked up from a late replay of *The Tonight Show*. "And what are those?" he asked.

"Thigh cuffs." Tony said. "I bought them at that kinky place with the sex toys and stuff. The one upstairs, across the street from the coffee shop where the muscle guys hang out. Want to give them a try?" They began laughing at the same time.

"Tomorrow night, OK? I'm nearly dead. Besides, now that we're officially getting married, we've got all the time in the world."

Santos dreamed his favorite dream that night. He and Tony walked up into the air as if climbing a gently sloping hill. They looked down on the houses and treetops. And then they began to fly as slowly or rapidly as they wished, whisked along above the world, looking down on the darkened streets and buildings, the probing headlights of cars. Together, hand in hand, flying under the moon and stars. Together, forever safe, unseen above the world.

At breakfast Tony regarded Santos over a twice-bitten piece of toast. "You know what?" A pile of orange marmalade teetered on the edge, then formed itself into a slimy avalanche that ran onto his fingers. Tony scooped the mess up with the tip of his tongue.

"What?" Santos asked.

"You woke me up last night, laughing in your sleep. You do that a lot."

Santos smiled. He wished they could stay here and never go back. But there were loose ends he had to tie up. And then they'd leave for good. They could come back here, or go anywhere they wanted. Finally, after years of dead ends and partial success, he had the money.

CHAPTER NINE

F ernie didn't really think of himself as a hustler, but the El Paso Police Department definitely did. He pulled his jacket collar up and stayed close to the phone. Whenever the police stopped—which happened often enough for him to know many of them by name—he told them he was waiting for a phone call from his sister. No one had passed a law yet that said a kid couldn't wait by a public phone for a call from his sister.

On weeknights, older-model cars and vans with business logos slowly cruised the street, circled the block, came back again, and pulled over to the curb with the engine still running. The vehicles usually had miniature saddles, tiny Stetson hats, or dream-catchers hanging from the mirrors. Some had religious medals or a tiny Virgin of Guadalupe or the Black Saint, San Martín, stuck to the dash. The men, who hungrily fucked him, did so silently and without preamble or protection. They were mostly older men with wedding rings they never bothered to remove, and—Fernie imagined—sons his age whose bodies they fantasized about using in the same way they used his. But they didn't regard themselves as homosexuals, and neither did Fernie.

In his sophomore year at Jeff, he got an erection while

showering with the boys in his gym class. That afternoon the guy whose budding chest hair and generous endowments had so excited him waited for him after school, accompanied by several of his friends, and they'd beaten Fernie severely. The next day the same clique beat him up again. After beating him for the third time in the same week, they stole his pants and underwear. He walked home, bloodied and bruised, wrapped in his shirt. Many of the neighbors saw him. His mother, sealed in shame, said nothing. His own father called him a *maricón* to his face, his voice clotted with loathing. Although he knew his truancy would be the last bit of leverage his father would need to throw him out, Fernie vowed not to go back to Jefferson High. "*No voy a lidiar con ningún joto,*" his father pronounced. That night after the family had retired Fernie packed the clothes that didn't remind him of school and split.

For the last couple of years he'd lived with his alcoholic sister and her *marimacha* girlfriend. Sleeping on their broken-down couch, he was a frequent witness to their violent fights and almost equally turbulent lovemaking. On weekend nights like tonight, he stayed all night on the street, making what he could, watching the men going to and from the area clubs. He shook a Marlboro from the crumpled pack, lit up, and watched the pair who had just come out of the Mining Company. Fernie stared openly at the older of the two. Definitely his type, Fernie decided. Something about the intimate familiarity of the way they moved together told Fernie the men were lovers.

The younger man talked excitedly. Fernie overheard him say something about San Francisco. The older guy, wearing a black leather jacket that matched his companion's, nodded and laughed in response. He was clearly happy to be with his partner. They both looked at Fernie as they approached, and smiled. The younger guy asked him how he was. Fernie smiled back. Most of the guys from the club ignored him or at most just glanced at him and hurried by in silence. Fernie figured they were just glad not to *be* him. He flicked his partially smoked cigarette onto the sidewalk and ground it out under his heel. He wished he had a lover and that they were headed for the OP to dance the world away. He hoped he lived that long. He stood watching the pair as they walked down the street together, almost touching shoulders. He didn't notice the dark Camaro as it slithered around the corner of San Antonio and Ochoa, still a block away, headed in his direction.

| ✶ |

"So relax, OK? These are fags, for fuck sake. It's no problem, OK? And if there is, which is un-fucking-likely, you got Ron here as backup."

Neal Pearson figured Lyle had addressed this pep talk primarily to him, since Ron had already chambered a round and left the hammer back. Neal's hands shook as he worked the slide. He sat up straight with the pistol held down between his knees, the muzzle pointed at the floor. Just like he'd been instructed. Seen from the street, he looked just like any other passenger.

"When we get up to that sign, we'll pick a target," Lyle continued. "We'll take somebody right in front of the fucking place. That way we'll be positive."

"What about him?" Ron pointed to the Hispanic kid loitering by the public phone.

Lyle thought about it. "Nah," he answered. "Can't be sure. He might just be some kid." Lyle pulled the car to the corner and stopped.

"Them!" Ed shouted, pointing at two men walking side-by-side in the block ahead. "Right there! Look at how they're walking, goddamn it. No mistake about *that!* Fucking faggots!"

"Yeah, they're good ones, all right. You guys ready back there? Here goes!" Lyle began to pull across the intersection.

"Just line us up, buddy." Ron rolled his window down. "Move over here, Neal, so you can shoot. Got your plugs in?"

Neal just nodded. He didn't trust his voice.

The car came to a halt, even with the strolling pair. The bigger of the two men seemed to sense the danger. He began to turn toward the Camaro.

"Hey, queers! Look what I've got!" Ron squeezed off the first round. "Shoot, goddamn it!" he shouted.

Neal raised the pistol and fired. Even with the ear plugs, the sound inside the car was deafening. His first shot missed the men and exploded harmlessly into the side of the dumpster behind them.

"Hell, yeah!" Ron roared, firing round after round in a frenzy. "Fucking faggots!"

The first shot hit Tony. He was closest to the curb. Santos lunged toward him, but he was too late to put himself between his lover and the barking white bursts of flame. He felt Tony's body thrown against his as the first round tore into the small of the boy's back. Tony's legs buckled. Santos strained to hold him up and drag him to safety. Several rounds slapped into the dumpster on the sidewalk behind them. A shot hit Santos below the right arm and passed through his upper back. The next hit Tony in his left buttock. Another bullet punched into Tony's chest. Santos felt him gasp. Tony clutched at him. "Help me...please...Santos..."

Santos felt Tony's fingers loosen, break away, slide down, the boy's weight sagging in his arms. Santos waited for the shot that would kill him too—ready to pay for his failure. Wishing it. He staggered backward. Something slammed his head into the side of the dumpster. He couldn't see. The metal tolled as another round slammed into it. He slipped slowly to the sidewalk with Tony sprawled on top of him. "Santos...help me."

"I'm here. I've got you." He tried to wipe the blood from his eyes but it flooded back again, blinding him as his consciousness slipped away.

Fernie stood rooted, hearing the shots from the Camaro without registering any sense of personal danger. His hand clasped over his mouth, he watched the younger guy fall heavily against his lover as the gunfire cut them down. Fernie watched as the patrons in front of the bar ducked for cover between parked cars, the events before him unfolding in slow motion, frame by frame. Then the assassins' car sped away, tires squealing, blue-white smoke billowing behind. At the intersection with Paisano, the car ran a red light and disappeared around the corner.

After the shooting stopped, several moments passed before the people on the street began to react. Somewhere down the street, a woman screamed. Fernie saw the front door of the OP burst open as two security guards ran out, looking around in momentary confusion. Nearby, a siren shrilled as a police black-and-white wheeled into the intersection, the wail descending to a growl as the car lurched to a stop. The cop inside spoke into the radio, then opened the door—in no apparent hurry—and got out.

Fernando ran toward the fallen men.

"Yo!" the cop shouted, holding up his hand.

Fernie kept coming.

The cop stepped forward threateningly. "I'm telling you to stay the hell back, you little fag!"

"Help them!" Fernie shouted. Then he recognized the cop. "*Ojete de la chingada!*" he hissed.

"An ambulance is coming," the cop snarled. "Now stay the hell back, or I'll arrest your faggot ass!" The cop turned his broad back to Fernie and walked casually over to where the bodies of the two men lay entangled, extracting his flashlight from his belt. Fernie followed him at a distance. The younger guy looked dead already. Blocks away, another siren shrilled and within minutes more flashing lights probed the shadows of the street. His fists clenched, Fernie watched while hot tears of rage ran down his cheeks.

CHAPTER TEN

Mr. De La O?" He opened his eyes. Martha Robles, his nurse, stood over his bed. Concern and sympathy seemed permanently stamped into her pleasant features. Martha had only recently graduated from her nursing program and had not yet taken her board exam. He'd overheard as much from the casual exchanges between Martha and the other staff nurses. He found Martha's inexperience reassuring. They probably weren't expecting his recovery to pose any challenge a new nursing graduate couldn't handle. That, at least, was what he hoped. "Some people from the police are here to see you," Martha said, her look of concern deepening.

He blinked a couple of times to clear his eyes. His hours in surgery had left him groggy, floating through events. He really had no idea what time it was. A bulky man with a square Mexican face, looking ill at ease in his rumpled suit, stood behind Martha. Next to him stood a tall woman with a spare, almost mannish frame and salt and pepper hair. The woman spoke first.

"Mr. De La O? I'm Detective Lessing. El Paso Police Department. This is my partner, Detective Acevedo." The square Mexican face remained expressionless. "We're sorry about your friend."

His friend. The reality of what the doctors had told him began to sink in. There would be no more life together with Tony. His friend.

"We need to ask you a few questions if you feel up to it," Lessing continued.

Santos nodded at the woman, at a complete loss for words.

"Did you see the people who did this?"

Had he? He must have, of course, but all he remembered was the weight of Tony's body falling against him. And a ringing sound, like the sound of church bells. Of course that couldn't be true.

But he could still hear it, all the same. Even in his sleep.

"I guess I did," he managed. "It's just that I don't seem to remember much about the...uh...about it." His mouth felt dry. He wished he had some water.

"The doctors warned us that you might not recall much. You received a pretty serious blow to the head."

"Do you recall seeing their car?" The other detective spoke for the first time. His voice contained much less sympathy than his partner's.

Santos thought about it for a moment. He couldn't will himself to see the car. He could only remember the muzzle blast, blooming again and again like a deadly white flower. He shook his head. The cops didn't care about muzzle blast.

"Do you know anyone who would want to do something like this to you, Mr. De La O?" Detective Lessing this time.

Santos had asked himself that question already, of course. Would the cartel have tried to hit him to help cover up their acquisition of the missiles? That was certainly possible. And killing him in front of a gay bar might make the shooting look like a drive-by hate crime. But how could they be sure he hadn't foreseen an attempt on his life as a possibility and made arrangements to expose what he knew about them in the event of his untimely death? Would they take that risk? Probably, he thought. Wasn't taking risks fundamental to the business. And betrayal? Wasn't betrayal the only certainty? "I'm not sure," he answered. "I can't think of anyone."

Lessing placed her business card on his bedside table. "If you remember anything, you'll let us know, Mr. De La O?"

Santos nodded.

"We'll be in touch. We hope you have a speedy recovery."

"Thanks," he said.

"We'll need you to positively identify your friend," Lessing's partner added. "Unless there's family who can do it."

"No, no family," Santos replied. "I'll do it."

"The docs say you should be out in a day or two. We'll check back with you then." The cops left. Santos twisted onto the side that hurt the least and buried his face in the pillow.

"Not much to say," Lessing observed as she and Acevedo waited for the elevator. "Usually they can't wait for someone to listen to them."

"He ain't looking for a shoulder to cry on," Chuy observed flatly. "He's hiding something. He's scared of someone." A *ding* announced the arrival of the elevator. The detectives squeezed into the crowded box and rode down in silence.

| ☆ |

Santos watched as Detective Acevedo stopped at the window and rapped the glass with his wedding ring. He and the two detectives stood waiting, trying to avoid looking at each other. Santos stared at the toes of his worn brown hiking shoes and at the shallow path the passage of countless feet had eroded into the linoleum tiles. A rust-colored splatter that had been incompletely mopped away formed a smear up the pale-green tile wall. Acevedo glanced at him again obliquely and rapped the glass harder. A skinny dreadlocked man in threadbare green scrubs came to the window and pushed a thick green ledger through the slot in the glass partition. Acevedo scribbled his signature, told him which body they'd come to identify, and pushed the ledger back. The attendant buzzed them in. Santos felt Lessing touch his arm through his sling.

"This isn't going to be pleasant, Mr. De La O." She removed her hand self-consciously, sensing that De La O didn't wish to be touched.

Dreadlocks led them to a series of stacked metal shelves set into the far wall, consulting a clipboard as he walked. He paused at intervals to peer at the serried rows of numbered tabs, then stopped and reached for a handle, about to yank the drawer open.

Acevedo frowned at the attendant and shook his head as he eased his bulk around the obstacle of his partner and positioned himself at Santos's side. "Are you ready for this, sir?" he asked.

Santos nodded silently.

The latch clicked and the drawer slid out noiselessly, freeing a draft of cold air and the sullen butcher-shop smell of refrigerated carcass.

Acevedo looked Santos full in the face for the first time since they'd arrived at the morgue. "You OK, sir?" The guy had just got out of the hospital. He'd nearly been shot to death himself. Even Chuy would concede that much.

"Yeah. I'll be all right. Let's get this done."

Chuy eased the sheet back gently from the face, relieved there had been no reason for the M.E. to open up the boy's head. He looked at the civilian. The man had gone a dead shade of gray in the face, turned his head to one side, and closed his eyes.

"Take a deep breath," Acevedo suggested.

De La O nodded and complied, opening his eyes and visibly willing himself to look at the body in the tray.

Chuy glanced across the tray at Jen. This guy was pretty tightly wrapped. Of the many things he hated about this job, bringing civilians down here to I.D. stiffs had to be near the top of the list. The fainting, the puking and the crying of the *bolillos* were nothing compared to the pure low-class histrionics of *cholos*, from the women especially, always accompanied by at least a busload of relatives, the men among them invariably reeling drunk. Screaming, recriminations, scuffles that turned into all out brawls. Right in the presence of the dearly departed.

Chuy Acevedo hated *cholos* more than anyone, hated them with the cold fury of a man betrayed by his own family. Coming down here with their hair nets and bandannas, their pants hanging off their asses. Making their stupid gang signs with tattooed fingers and calling the dead guy "homes" and "*ése*." Chuy hated them worst of all. Dead already, all of them, as far as he was concerned. He'd once heard a black comedian say, "As soon as blacks start making some progress, some nigger comes along and fucks it up." He'd been surprised at how well it captured the way he felt—except for him it was the gangbangers who'd come along and wiped their asses on all of *la raza*, on people like him who had clawed their way up against all odds. For now, he swallowed his revulsion. The civilian was right. They needed to I.D. this DOA and get on with it.

"Can you identify him?" Acevedo asked.

"Yes. Can I have just a minute alone?"

The cops exchanged a glance. "Sure," Lessing said. She gave a slight inclination of her head toward a corner and walked away with Detective Acevedo in tow.

Lessing watched De La O from the corner. He was tall for

a Mexican. Light-skinned. And buff. But then lots of guys these days were buff, and lots of Mexicans were light-skinned and tall. Something about De La O reminded her of her father, and of her firearms instructor at the academy. He possessed the same toughness, the same competence. He looked like he'd come out well in a fight. "I wonder what he wants with him?" she asked her partner.

"Probably wants to drop one last load in his ass before they bury him," Acevedo muttered under his breath.

Lessing whispered something Acevedo didn't quite catch.

"Say again?" he asked.

"I said, it's not necessary to be gross."

"Talk to the fags if you got a problem with gross, Detective. I'm just stating a simple fact." He groped in his coat pocket for his smokes, tapped one out, lit it, and inhaled deeply. He watched the civilian through the smoke as he inhaled again, the effort drawing his nostrils into hard little slits.

Lessing had gotten her answer. Chuy clearly had a thing about homosexuals. If this case ever got solved, it would not likely be due to any great effort on his part.

"Butt boys," Acevedo grumbled to no one in particular. "Sick pieces of shit taking it up the ass." The tip of the cigarette flared cherry red again. He dropped it to the floor and ground it out under his shoe. "Fucking AIDS cases."

Santos pulled the sheet down to Tony's knees. The gold chain and crucifix he always wore were gone. The fatal wound gaped in the high right side of the chest, under the armpit. He picked up Tony's right hand and examined the long, thin fingers. A barely visible half moon shone its pale, dead light at the origin of each fingernail. A juvenile trait. Tony's hand felt like something rubber that had been left out in the cold. He touched a slender thigh, the meat dead, hanging on the bone. The penis and scrotum hung down loosely between his scrawny legs with thighs that never touched, even at the top. Under the legs he could see a small pool of rust colored blood. Even after he'd been autopsied, he'd bled.

"*Me tocas en lo vivo*," Santos whispered to the inert form in the tray.

He placed his hand gently on the chest, lightly caressing the notch at the base of the neck, recognizing the gesture even as he did it as a futile attempt at consolation. He'd been late, so very, very late. Now the impossibly broken apparatus that had been Antonio, his lover, the light in his heart, lay cold and impassive, as far beyond life as the ashes the body would soon become.

Ignoring the sharp pain the motion caused, he leaned over the body. Almost overpowered by its putridly sweet odor, he kissed his fingertips and pressed them gently against the empty face. Someone had closed the unseeing eyes.

"*Te amo...te amo tanto, tanto.* I love you. I love you so very much." He stood staring at the wreckage of his happiness. And would have stayed there for hours, if Detective Lessing hadn't spoken.

"Sorry, Mr. De La O. We'll need to be getting along soon."

He looked over at the beefy Hispanic cop and his tall *bolilla* sidekick, hardly able to bring them into focus. Then he looked for the last time at Tony. "*Yo te vengaré. Te lo juro,*" he whispered. "I will avenge you. I swear it."

Santos pulled the sheet back up, slid the tray in along its smoothly gliding rails, and carefully closed the door.

Lessing startled involuntarily as the stainless steel latch snapped shut.

| ★ |

On her own time, Lessing had talked the case around the Crimes Against Persons Division, looking for resources. She'd interviewed the male couple who ran the Rainbow Services Coalition and a spokesman for *Adelante!*, a local Hispanic gay advocacy group. Not surprisingly, the gay men knew more about hate crimes against their community than anyone at the police department. The data they'd collected showed a clear picture. Violence against gays and lesbians had risen steeply in the past two years and had become more directly expressed, more personalized. In the past, rocks, bottles, and epithets had been slung from passing cars. Now the majority of assaults involved fists, baseball bats, knives and pieces of pipe—weapons that called for face-to-face confrontation. The black cross-dresser had been well-known in the community. But no one Lessing interviewed seemed to know anything about the boy who had been murdered, or his partner.

To Jen, the two most recent assaults only *seemed* different: the first a beating, the second a shooting. But both were executions, carried out with hideous, almost ritualistic, savagery. Only two weeks separated the crimes. And each had been committed by more than one person. That, at least, seemed clear.

The cross-dresser in the park had been attacked with a weapon forensics had not been able to identify, and kicked repeatedly—probably with steel-toed boots, given that the internal organs had been reduced to pulp. Although no eyewitnesses to the assault had come forward, it seemed unlikely to Jen that so much damage had been inflicted by a single assailant, no matter how psychotic or enraged.

In the case of the two men gunned down in front of the Old Plantation, the situation was clearer. There had definitely been more than one shooter. Both the witnesses and the ballistic evidence supported it. At the time of the attack, the men had been walking in front of a dumpster left on the sidewalk to be emptied the next morning. Behind the dumpster was the soft stucco wall of a building. The rounds that hit the dumpster had disintegrated. Ballistics couldn't even establish their caliber with certainty. But the rounds extracted from the wall had been essentially intact. Eight more rounds, several intact, had been recovered from the bodies of the victims. The intact bullets preserved two different barrel signatures. Which meant at least two pistols, and therefore two shooters. Maybe a driver, too.

Lessing felt sure the recent murders reflected team efforts, but if they had been committed by the same group, why had the killers changed their approach? Could they be trying to conceal their identity? Texas, she had learned, was a state widely identified with hate crimes. Were there hate groups in this area who targeted gays? No one she'd talked to in the police department seemed to know, or appeared interested in finding out. So she made a call to the department of political science at the local University of Texas, and another to the same specialty at New Mexico State University.

CHAPTER ELEVEN

Santos parked in the basement and slipped the nine millimeter Sig from its customized holster mounted under the vehicle's dash. He folded the previous day's *Diario de Juárez* over the gun, and tucked the bundle under his arm with the butt of the pistol facing forward in the event he needed it. He rode the elevator up to the apartment he'd rented. Since the shooting, he'd felt paranoid. He'd moved out of the house he'd shared with Tony and put the furniture in consignment.

Santos mixed himself a hefty black Russian, turned on the CD player for the first time since Tony's death, and stepped out onto the balcony. From the open doorway Daniela Romo sang "*Si Dios me quita la vida,*" her voice rising over the lonely notes of muted trumpets. He took a long swallow and felt the vodka burn through him. Sixteen days had passed since the owner of a local mortuary had given Santos his condolences and handed him an anonymous gray container of grit.

For all Santos cared, the dull metal urn could have held nothing more than sand from the bed of some nameless arroyo high in the desert. What possible relation could these pitiful calcined bone fragments have to his memories of Tony? How could he connect ashes to private smiles of complicity, to Tony's high and perfect voice singing Juanga's ranchero music in the shower while he exhausted the city's supply of hot water, or to the rutting smell of late night lust mingled with cool morning air? Santos looked out over the city, wondering why these connections eluded him, but more than anything hating the world's indifference to the death of its parts.

He nursed his drink and stared out across the skyline. The sky had blackened. Distant thunder from behind the mountains promised imminent rain. A towering nimbus of light enveloped the banks and hotels at the city's center, then flattened and spread outward to the rim of the wide valley, a great lake of light in the blackness of a desert that stretched for hundreds of miles in all directions. The green-black glass surface of the county courthouse caught and distorted the lights from the taller buildings. Tony's murderers would never stand there in that dark palace of justice. According to his discreet inquiries, the cops weren't even looking for them. Cops, Santos assumed, weren't much interested in fags. Announced by a roll of thunder, fat drops of rain began to fall.

Santos constructed himself another black Russian and stood for a long while by the patio doors, lulled by the patter of fine drizzle, absently watching silver rivulets writhe their way down the glass. He undressed in the dark and dropped onto the coolness of the empty bed. Eventually the choking, animal sounds of his grief yielded to the jagged breathing of his dreams. In his sleep he lost Tony again and again, night after night, too late, too late, eternally too late. He awoke after each nightmare shaking and covered with sweat, cut to the bone by guilt.

| ✻ |

Jackie Boyles entered the Taconazo in a foul mood, clumped over to the booth where Santos sat waiting, and dropped her square frame into the seat opposite him.

"Thanks for coming," he said.

"I'm having a shitty day here," she hissed. "For starters, I shouldn't even be here. And I definitely should not be doing what I'm doing right now. If anyone finds out I copped this file, I could get my ass suspended from the force. For good. And God knows what else, which I don't even want to think about."

"And how would anyone find out?" Santos replied. "I'll bet you found that file buried under a stack at least two feet deep."

"Wrong." Jackie glanced around the restaurant, relieved that at least they were sitting in a back corner booth, away from the window. "I took it off Detective Jenna Lessing's desk. It was definitely not in the inactive can, which is where I personally would have expected it to be, knowing the police department as I do. But that's not exactly the point. You're not an attorney. You are not in any way an officer of the court. You are not, as far as I am aware, a licensed anything. You're Italian, right? So that means you're not even related to this person."

"My father's side is Italian. And you're right, I'm not a licensed anything. Aside from my freedom, I have nothing the great state of Texas can revoke. How about some lunch? The food here's good."

"Sure, why not? I might as well get something out of this."

Santos caught the waitress's eye, and they placed their orders.

"You've already gotten something from it," Santos said. "You're paid up. Now tell me, why do you think Lessing is interested in this case?"

"Don't jerk me around, Santos. People like me never get paid up." Boyles stared at him angrily, clearly not buying his reassurances.

"I spoke to my boss personally this morning. I told him I needed a favor. Besides, they owe me. You're off the hook. Account closed. Paid," he reiterated.

Jackie's shoulders dropped with relief.

"I'm only doing what you guys do every day," he said. "Calling in favors. It's business. Just business."

"Favor, my ass. Fucking blackmail!" she spat.

"Semantics, Jackie. Now answer my question. Why the interest in this case?"

"How should I know? I don't live in the woman's mind. Besides, she's new. And she's not from here. She and her doctor husband moved here from the East Coast someplace. How should I know why this blows her dress up? She's probably some liberal do-gooder schmuck." Jackie paused. Their waitress put down two orders of beef and chicken fajitas. "Besides, somebody will set her straight soon enough about how we don't do things here. Probably that asshole partner of hers." Jackie lit into the steaming plate. "I'll tell you something else," she said, talking around her food. "She also had the file on that transvestite that got whacked in the park downtown."

"She thinks Tony's murder was connected to another killing?"

"Here," she said. "Take this shit. Please." She shoved a nine-by-thirteen manila envelope, folded lengthwise, across the table. Santos slipped it into the pocket of his jacket. "So, what's your interest in this kid?" she asked.

"He was my lover." Santos noticed her jaw set.

Boyles nodded several times, her eyes narrowing as the implications played out in her mind. "Well, Jesus fuck us to tears," she muttered. She sipped her coffee, watching him over the rim of her cup. "Well," she continued after several moments of silence, "I hope he gets some kind of justice. 'Cause I know where these cases end up if the department handles them. This kind of stuff just melts away. They just look busy and wait for people to forget, which usually doesn't take very long."

She returned to her coffee and looked across the table at him. "I'm sorry, Santos, but that's how it is. And, yes, I would guess Lessing thinks the killings are related. I mean, think about it, Santos. In a town this size, what are the odds of two things like this happening back-to-back? Not even in J-town would this pass for coincidence. Unless, of course, the cops did it." Her voice contained no trace of irony. Everyone knew what the Mexican police were capable of.

"Yes," he said softly. "I'm aware. So how's it going with you and Janine?"

"Oh, that," she answered flatly. "Fuck that, I can tell you. I can catch 'em left and right, but I'll be goddamned if I can keep 'em." The waitress came to refill Jackie's coffee. Jackie briskly stirred a triple sugar into it. "I don't know why I even got into this for her. Protecting that coke-head cunt. She's as crazy as the proverbial shithouse rat. She's probably stopped embezzling from her employers and started selling her ass for it by now."

"Well, for what it's worth, I'm sorry to hear it," Santos lied. He had no sympathy for anyone who lived in copworld. But it would be impolitic, not to mention counterproductive, for him to remind Jackie that it had been Jackie Boyles shaking down dealers to keep Janine supplied, and that Jackie Boyles was the person with whom Jackie Boyles had always been most in love, not Janine the Junkie, "wasted dispose-a-cunt" as Jackie herself had once described her in a rare moment of lucidity.

"And I thank you for that sentiment. Really." She slid across the seat and rose to leave.

"You're not going to finish?" he asked.

"No thanks. Suddenly, I'm not all that hungry. You won't be either after you've read that report."

"I was there, Jackie. I don't need to read the report."

"That's not exactly what I meant. Anyway, you'll figure it out when you read it. You take care, Santos."

"Sure, thanks. You too, Jackie."

"Yeah, I'll be sure and do that. Oh...and Santos?" He looked up at her. "Whatever you do—and I assure you I don't give a flying fuck what it is—either do it in some other jurisdiction or on someone else's shift, OK? 'Cause me, I'm up to my tomboy tits in paperwork already. Really."

"You know, Jackie, one of my uncles has a saying. *Tutti i nodi vengano al pettine. Capisci?*"

"And what's that supposed to mean?"

"All the snags come to the comb," he answered.

"I don't get it."

"What goes around comes around."

"Yes, that it does," she replied.

] ✶ [

The intercom buzzer woke Santos from a restless sleep. He rolled out of bed, grabbed a pair of jeans off the floor, and pulled them on. He tucked in his erection, careful to avoid the zipper. "Who is it?" he asked.

"Mr. De La O?" The tinny voice seemed familiar.

"Yes?"

"Detective Lessing. I'd like to speak with you. Is this a bad time?"

"Uh, sure. I'll buzz you in." He waited by the door until he heard the elevator arrive. A moment later Lessing knocked. Santos checked his jeans for any inappropriate bulges and opened the door.

"Woke you up, I guess. Bad timing." Today she wore a simply cut gray suit. It accentuated the gray in her hair but without making her seem old.

"No problem. I just fell asleep." How had she managed to find him? All the police had was his old address.

"So, how are you doing?" she asked.

He realized the question had been put seriously, not simply as an attempt to be polite. "Making it, I guess. A day at a time. I moved. I guess you noticed."

"Rarely a problem," she smiled. "Phone companies maintain current addresses, and the post office has forwarding addresses. They're required to share with us."

"So, have you come to tell me you've found the guys who killed my lover?" He put the ball in her court now, to see how she'd react to his description of Tony.

"No, I'm sorry to say. I wanted to come by to talk to you before I interviewed our other witnesses. Most of the people who saw the attack chose not to get involved, unfortunately. Other than the witnesses the investigating officer spoke to that night, no one else has come forward. As yet," she added.

"I see. Well, why don't you have a seat. Coffee?"

"Sure, if you're having some. That would be great. Black, please." Lessing adjusted her spare frame to the sofa and surveyed the sparsely furnished apartment while Santos ground fresh beans and worked the coffee machine. Too generic, no personality. That would make it rental furniture. "So what is it exactly that you do?" she asked, breaking the silence.

"I'm in the export business," she heard him say over the gurgle and clatter of coffee making.

"Really? That sounds interesting. What is it you export?"

"Nothing at the moment. I'm between jobs, actually."

Change of subject duly noted. She decided to let it ride for now.

"Do you have any leads on the guys who did this?"

Suddenly it was Lessing's turn to get evasive. "We have some information we're working on. You still don't recall seeing their car?"

"No, I've tried, but I can't get it back. What did the other witnesses have to say about it?" He'd reentered the living room with two steaming mugs of coffee. He handed her one.

"Thanks. Well," she conceded, "the only other eyewitness at this point is a middle-aged woman who sells food out of the trunk of her car."

"Yeah, I remember seeing her. She's out there every weekend."

"She described it as a sports car but didn't know the make. Unfortunately, the car turned the corner before the bar's security made it out to the street. I was thinking that you seem like the kind of guy who would know sports cars." Lessing sipped her coffee approvingly and waited for his response.

"I drive an older model Jeep, actually."

"Or Jeeps," she added. "There's one thing I need from you. It's personal, but it could help me a lot when I talk to witnesses. I'd like a picture of you and your partner, if that wouldn't be too much of an imposition." She looked at him expectantly. Would he agree?

"Sure." What could it hurt? He went to the bedroom and returned with a picture in a frame. He deftly removed the picture and tossed the empty frame on the couch. He handed the picture to Lessing. "Here you go."

"Thanks," she said, tucking the photo gently into her purse. "I promise to take good care of it."

Lessing entered the elevator and punched the button for the lobby. When the doors slid open, though, she stayed aboard and rode the car down to the basement garage. In the underground parking lot she scanned the lines of vehicles until she spotted the battered Jeep. She looked it over quickly, jotted down the tag number, and took the stairs back up to the street. If Santos came down the elevator for some reason, she didn't want to meet him.

These apartments seemed pretty swank for someone between jobs. Could De La O be hiding from someone? A former employer perhaps? The shooting appeared to be a hate crime, but she'd decided to take nothing for granted about this case. After all, this was El Paso, the southwest's busiest conduit for illegal people, exotic animals, and drugs. Not all international exchange here consisted of pretty Mexican pottery and handwoven blankets.

CHAPTER TWELVE

T he breakfast crowd at Jaxon's had thinned and the first wave of the early lunch crowd had not yet materialized. Santos sat in the privacy of the upstairs section, at the far end by the windows. He ordered coffee and runny eggs over hash browns, and waited until the server had disappeared into the kitchen before he emptied the contents of the manila envelope onto the table. He slid the glossy color photos from forensics back into the envelope without looking at them. He'd made that mistake yesterday, and had spent the afternoon trying to drown his anger and remorse in a bottle. Beginning with the autopsy report on Tony, he turned his attention to the paperwork. Finally he turned to the document of greatest interest, the hastily typed police report.

The police response had been initiated by a 911 call, logged in at 22:57, about two hours after dark. The call had been placed by the first officer to arrive at the scene, from the street in front of the club where he and Tony had been headed at the time of the attack. The name of a club security man appeared on the report, followed by the man's address and phone number. The name of a second person, Fernando Fernandez, identified simply as a "bystander," listed an address, no phone number. Apparently Fernandez was the only person interviewed by the police to have actually witnessed the attack. Santos made a mental note. Finding Fernandez and talking to him would be his first priority.

The impressions of the witnesses were summarized in the first few paragraphs of the report. The body of the report recapitulated what the police had found at the scene. No empty casings had been found in the street. The report surmised that the spent cartridges had been contained within the perp's vehicle as they were ejected from the guns. Using a car as a brass catcher had the double advantage of leaving less evidence and of supplying a means of instant escape. It showed premeditation.

Aside from the lead to Fernandez, the report revealed little of specific interest. Witnesses had seen two, possibly more, white males, a dark sports car, no tag number. That narrowed the suspects down to a few million, Santos reflected bitterly. None of the security people had actually seen the shooting, having been made aware of it by a patron entering the club. Given the noise inside, the security men had not even heard the shots. A woman who sold tamales from the trunk of her car had seen the vehicle, but knew nothing about makes and models. The report made no mention of attackers shouting epithets. In some jurisdictions, the police routinely asked about that sort of thing. But in Texas hate crimes carried no more jail time than simple assaults in which the perpetrator was presumed to have no feelings one way or another about the skin color, religious beliefs, or sexual orientation of the mark he'd just fucked over.

Santos put down the file and sipped his coffee, half watching the late morning flux of people. A conversation sprinkled with laughter bubbled along in another corner of the restaurant. Until that moment, he'd been completely unaware of it. He slipped the papers back into the envelope. Jackie had been correct. The report was brief and barren to the point of perfunctory. It had recorded only the most basic elements, a mere sketch of the shooting. No individual descriptions, no mention of clothing, no real description of the car. A typical example of *mevalemadrismo*, the what-the-fuck attitude that pervaded the town.

Santos had tried repeatedly to recall the details of the shooting, and failed. Maybe it was the groove cut into his skull, or the sedation he'd received in the hospital, or the period of anesthesia in the operating room. Or just plain shock. "Retrograde amnesia," the doctors had called it. Just a fancy term for not being able to remember what had happened. He did remember the white flashes of muzzle blast, the weight of Tony in his arms, the endless fall to the pavement, and Tony's final call for help—as if heard from afar. Aside from these fragments of memory, strobe lit by his sense of failure, the rest of the event had no more substance than a ball of lint.

He knew that any murder not solved within a few days would likely never be satisfactorily closed. Contrary to the kind of police work reported on television, in the majority of homicide cases resolved by police investigation the killer was either well known to police, still at the scene, or identified by name by witnesses—usually family, friends, or close neighbors known to the victim. Tracking down the killer generally amounted to picking him up drunk at his mother's house, his girlfriend's apartment, or his favorite bar. The occasional shithead might blunder into a confession of murder while being questioned on some other charge: "I couldn't have raped that chick because I was killing a guy at the time." As a rule, once a month had gone by, only an accomplice or a cellmate trying to cut a deal for a sentence reduction somewhere down the line would put a guy's balls in the wringer. Santos would have bet that half the unidentified murderers in the country were already in prison anyway, jailed on drug or robbery charges.

In the majority of murder cases, he'd learned, the police provided a show of force and kept agitated family members and neighbors at bay while EMS hauled away the injured and the dead. In some neighborhoods, police protection of firefighters and ambulance crews who responded to 911 calls were small scale military deployments. In Tony's case, the police department had limited itself to removing the body and the routine filling out of papers. The cops had doughnuts to eat, coffee to drink, and ticket quotas to meet. Most seasoned officers took a sensible approach to the job, avoided people with guns and attitudes as much as possible, and tried to retire with a complete inventory of body parts and a few shreds of sanity. Leave the high-pressure murder investigations to the guys on TV.

Cop culture had worked to Santos's advantage many times before, and might again. Despite Lessing's appearance at his apartment, the odds were that interest in the case would soon fade, replaced by more recent killings. After all, attacks on queers happened every other day.

| ✱ |

The usual background noises of the department had ebbed. Most of the desks were already empty, their occupants home eating supper with family. Lessing keyed up the screen for the Department of Motor Vehicles and tapped in the plate number from the Jeep. The computer searched its memory for a few moments before another screen appeared. The Jeep was registered to one Jesús Goncalva. The mailing address listed a post office box. Lessing gazed at the screen for a few seconds, then rechecked the number. The number in her notebook matched the number on the screen. There had been no mistake.

She exited the screen, typed "Santos De La O" on a different screen, and waited for it to process. The data bank matched two names. One, a 55-year-old man, lived in San Angelo. The other, a 16-year-old boy, had just been issued a learner's permit. Lessing leaned back in her chair and shook her head, a wry smile slowly forming around her eyes and mouth. Alias Jesus and the Saints. Whatever the exact nature of Mr. De La O's exporting business, she'd at least give him credit for a sense of humor.

She removed the portrait of Santos and Tony from the top drawer of her desk, carefully covered Tony's image so it wouldn't copy, and sent off a high-resolution fax of Santos's face to the Federal Bureau of Investigation. The Bureau would feed the face into its sophisticated data bank. Their computers would first measure the features of the photo precisely and then search for any possible match. With any luck, she'd hear something back within 24 hours. Her inquiry into the kid's murder had turned into an investigation of his lover, she realized. But she was determined to go with what she had.

She'd tried several times to interview the kid Fernando Fernandez, the only eyewitness who had come forward, but to no avail. Fernandez, it seemed, had left town to visit relatives in Mexico. When might he be back? "Who knows?" his mannish sister had shrugged. "Maybe *el día de mañana*." And *mañana*, Chuy had told her emphatically, did not mean "tomorrow." It meant "not today."

CHAPTER THIRTEEN

S teep, cracked concrete steps nearly lost between over-grown hedges and weeds snaked up to the house. The heat of the early afternoon sun burned down on Santos as he slogged his way up through the blue-gray haze of smog. Somewhere in a yard down the street, a man and woman argued loudly in shrill, rapid-fire Spanish, the tone of their voices rising even faster than the temperature. He paused for a moment, out of habit, long enough to nail down the accent. Funny, he thought, most Salvadorans headed for L.A. As he resumed his climb, the monotonous drone of traffic from the freeway rose to fill the occasional lull in their shouting. The exertion made his recent injuries twinge.

The once white paint had begun to peel away in long strips from the weathered door frame. He checked the number again, 706, and knocked. The tin 6 had long since disap-peared, its fossil negative embedded like a prehistoric foot-print in the layers of oxidized paint. He waited a few minutes and knocked again. The curtain in the window beside the door moved slightly.

"*Quién es?*" asked a young male voice from behind the door.

"*Mi nombre es Santos. Santos De La O. Estoy intentando ponerme en contacto con Fernando Fernandez. Soy amigo del muchacho…este…el joven que mataron hace tres semanas.*"

"*Policía?*" the voice inquired.

"*No. En absoluto. No tengo nada que ver con la policía.*" Santos waited while locks and bars rattled on the other side of the door. A thin face with eyes so dark they looked black inspected him warily through a crack between the door and the jamb. The door closed again as the boy unfastened the final chain. The door reopened, a bit wider this time. Santos felt sure he'd seen this boy before, but couldn't place where.

"*Pásele, pues.*" The boy opened the door wider and motioned Santos in. "I'm Fernie," he continued, switching to perfect, unaccented English. "You want a beer?"

"Yeah, a beer would be great. Thanks." The boy wore a faded yellow undershirt and what looked like a woman's fly-less shorts. His skinny legs ended in delicate feet clad in worn-down, soiled flip-flops. Except for the conspicuous bulge in his shorts, the kid could have passed for 13.

"Please excuse the place. I live here with my sister and her girlfriend. *Son unas cochinas insoportables.*" Unbearable pigs. Santos smiled. "*Tome asiento,*" the boy said, motioning toward a battered sofa.

Santos sat as directed and was rewarded with a poke in the ass from a broken spring. He repositioned himself as inconspicuously as possible as the boy flip-flopped his way to the kitchen. Santos looked around in the half-light. The place was a dusty shambles and smelled like stale cat litter.

Fernando returned with two cans of light beer. He handed one to Santos, perched a pointy butt cheek on the threadbare arm of the couch, and regarded his guest with thinly disguised interest.

Santos sipped his beer and returned Fernie's stare. Suddenly he made the connection. "You're the kid by the phone!" Santos said.

"I'm not a kid," the man-child replied defensively. Then he asked, "You dig kids?" He gave Santos an insinuating half smile. "'Cause I could be *your* kid."

"I like guys. Not kids," Santos said, feeling a little unnerved by the boy's question. "I didn't mean to offend you. I just realized how your name got in the police report."

"I'm sorry you lost your lover," Fernie replied, suddenly serious. "You were a good couple. Anyone could see that." Like Detective Lessing's, the boy's voice contained real sympathy.

"Thanks for saying that. I guess I've needed to hear someone say that." Santos felt choked. He sipped the rapidly warming beer until he could trust his voice again. "The police report didn't have much information in it. I wondered if you could remember anything else about that night."

"Like what?" Fernie asked. "I remember lots about it."

"Well, a description of the car, for instance. The report said it was a sports car."

"Camaro," the boy replied. "Anybody could see that. There's a million of them here. I told them that. A Camaro, dark blue." Fernie sipped his beer. "It stopped right in the middle of the street while those guys shot...while they shot you and your boyfriend."

"Did you see the plates?" Santos asked, trying to keep hope from his voice. He had so little to go on. The color of the plates would at least tell what state had issued them. Texas plates had black lettering on white, most New Mexico plates were bright yellow, and plates from Mexico, which had changed recently, were also distinctive. He might at least be able to figure out the area from which the car had originated.

"*Con permiso*," the boy said, rising from his place at the end of the couch. He shuffled back into the kitchen and returned with a piece of paper and a stub of pencil. "Here, I'll write it for you." He scribbled something and handed Santos the piece of paper. "It's the tag number. I think it's some kind of vanity plate. From New Mexico. That's what made it easy to remember. But I told the cop that."

"Thanks," Santos said, momentarily unable to tear his eyes away from the paper in his hands. "You're sure you told this to the cops?"

"I already told you what I told the cop. I even wrote it down for him, the *pinche ojete.*"

Fernando clearly didn't like cops, Santos thought.

"I see lots of cars. I notice stuff. I'm not stupid."

"Yeah. Sorry. I mean, I know you're not. It's just that it didn't show up in the police report."

"Then he left it out, didn't he?" Fernie shot back, clearly angry, but apparently not surprised.

"I guess so." Santos sipped at his beer and considered whether to give Fernie his cell phone number. He might have more to gain than lose by keeping in touch with the boy. "Has anyone else from the police tried to talk to you?" he asked, following a hunch.

"Yeah, some *gringa* detective came looking for me. My sister told her I was visiting family in Mexico."

Our paths cross again, Santos thought, absorbing this intelligence."She leave a card?"

The boy rose from the couch wordlessly and moved toward the unused fireplace. He sorted through paper rubble piled on the mantel, returned to the couch, and handed Santos the fruits of his search.

Santos turned the business card over in his hand. As he'd suspected, it belonged to Jenna Lessing. Turning the card to its blank side, he took the pencil stub, wrote the number to his wireless phone, and gave it to Fernie. "If you decide to go out of town, or if you hear anything more from the police, will you give me a call?"

The boy examined the phone number. "As long as you're around, I'll take my chances in El Paso, *papi*."

Santos smiled at the compliment and rose to leave.

"You know," the boy added, "there was nothing you could have done."

"Sure there was. I could have been paying attention to the street. If I'd seen the car, I'd have known something was wrong, trust me." Santos walked to the door and turned back to face the boy. "But thanks for saying that. And thanks again for the information. I'll put it to better use than the cops did, I promise."

"You going to kill the guys who shot your lover?"

"I'll have to find them first, won't I?" Santos answered, unnerved for yet a second time.

"I'd kill that fucking cop instead. He's easy to find."

"Why do you say that?" Santos asked.

"He'd have stood around and let you bleed to death." Fernie's voice stayed even, but sparks of hatred glittered in his eyes.

Santos nodded, letting the implications sink in. Fernando Fernandez had turned out to be quite an interview. He hoped Lessing didn't find him, but something told him the chances of that happening were slim to none.

| ★ |

Santos set the double scotch beside the PC, booted up, and tapped his way into the files of New Mexico's Department of Public Safety. Trying to suppress his anticipation, he typed in "WLFSKNS" and hit the enter key. The hands of a tiny clock icon ticked on the screen while the machine searched its memory. In less than a minute, the file popped up. He stared at it for several minutes, as if mesmerized by his first real contact with his assailants, before he hit Print.

Fernie had given an officer a valid plate number and the color and model of the car right at the scene of the crime, information which could have been confirmed within minutes from a terminal in a patrol car or by a call to police dispatch. Instead, the information had been suppressed. Santos intended to discover why.

He nursed his drink and turned back to the police report. The signature of the officer who had filed it was illegible, but the rest of the report, which had, after a fashion, been typed, identified the responding officer as James Thomas Mallory. Something told Santos that Fernie had had other encounters with him. After all, Fernie had been very emphatic about Mallory being an asshole. And why had Mallory failed to follow up on the information Fernie gave him? Why had he omitted the plate number from his report?

Santos decided he'd shower off the day's grime then head back over to Fernie's place. Maybe the little wise guy knew more than he'd said about this cop Mallory. He left his drink unfinished on the desk by the computer. For the first time since the attack he felt a sense of hope that Tony's killers might be found.

CHAPTER FOURTEEN

Dr. Fred Lessing laid his medical journal aside and watched his wife smoke. She'd given it up three times already with the help of pills, patches, and gum, only to restart during times of stress. She sat by the side of the pool, staring absently into the depths of the steep arroyo that wound its way downhill behind the house, in the direction of the distant gleam of Sunland Park Mall. She held the cigarette away from herself and out of sight. Sneaking a drag here and there, she pretended this would be the only one.

Jenna Lessing was no doctor's wife in the commonly understood sense. She loathed country clubs, didn't need a personal trainer, and had no time for power shopping, gossip, invidious comparisons of cars, homes, antiques, private schools, or investments. They'd made a good life out here, but not the rich-doctor kind of life. Still, Fred's practice had started to take off. The only other eye surgeon on this side of town had semiretired, and Fred now did eight to 10 refractory procedures a week—not high volume by Phoenix standards, but given the poverty level of El Paso, a number he considered good. His results were excellent, his reputation growing. And reputation was the basis of any solid surgical practice.

Fred hauled his lean frame out of the recliner, made a clean dive into the deep end of the pool, and swam over to where his wife sat, grinding out the butt of her third cigarette of the morning. He pulled himself up far enough out of the water to rest his arms on the edge. "What's up?" he asked.

"Just chilling." She'd missed a lot of sleep lately. Out here in the sun, it showed. Her eyes looked hollow. And sad.

"That's not what I meant, and you know it," he said it without recrimination.

"There are a couple of cases we're working on that bother me," she replied. "I mean, beyond the usual wife-beaters whose women are afraid to press charges."

"Well, you already know my remedy for that," Fred said grimly. He hefted himself out of the pool and sat on the side. She was watching him, he noticed. Watching the water stream down his arms and back. He thought about last night. They weren't getting any younger, but they were as much in love as they'd ever been. "So what's different about these?"

"Somebody's murdering gay men." She'd tried for a neutral tone and failed. "Besides the killing that made the papers, there was another one. Downtown, in the park. A transvestite. Savage." She tapped another cigarette from the pack and lit it.

"Any ideas?" He watched the tip of the cigarette flare. She exhaled, closed her hazel eyes against the burn of the smoke. When she reopened them and looked at him, her eyes didn't look tired anymore. They looked angry.

"We've got nothing, basically. This fucking department couldn't find the corpse at a one-car funeral." Jen was ready to unload. "In the first place, my buddy Chuy isn't interested. He doesn't like homosexuals. Or maybe I should say he hates homosexuals. So what happens to them doesn't concern him, even if it's murder. He couldn't give a shit." She took another drag, a long one. "When I got back to the office last week, the file on the guys who were shot in front of the bar? Gone

CUT TO THE BONE

from my desk. Disa-fucking-peared!" She pulled deeply again, and turned her head away from Fred to exhale. "I even...get this now...I even called the local university and asked one of the poli-sci professors if anyone local keeps track of hate groups. He suggested I get in touch with some guy at the University of California in San Diego."

"San Diego?" Fred laughed. He lowered himself back into the pool and rested his arms on the side. "What would they know about loonies in El Paso?"

"They couldn't know less than the El Paso police department." She stood, peeled off the white terry-cloth robe, and announced, "I'm coming in. At least under water I can't smoke."

Fred watched as her body knifed through the surface and she swam to the other side without coming up for air. On some level this was still about Jack, he realized. Jen's cousin, Jack Margolis, had been the best kid Fred could ever recall meeting. Good at heart, cheerful, bright, and, in a word, innocent. In Jack's junior year in high school, he'd been beaten senseless by a gang of men, two of whom had turned out to be students at the local college. They'd called him a cocksucking Jew faggot while they kicked his teeth out. During his months in rehab, Jack learned to walk and feed himself again. His sunny disposition returned, but the light had gone out. He never went back to school, never fulfilled his parents' brightest hopes, and even a year later he still sometimes soiled himself. The year after Jack had been assaulted, his younger sister, Melody, committed suicide. And after that his parents divorced. The entire family had been ravaged, their view of the world and of each other tarnished.

That was about the time Jen entered the Boston police academy, and Fred knew it was no coincidence. Jack had been Jenna's favorite, her confidante, closer to her than her own brothers. After what happened to Jack, Jen too had changed.

At the academy, she knocked her martial arts instructor out cold. She also finished first in her class and was the first to make detective. She had determination, the hardness the job demanded, but listened to her intuition. Fred had taught himself not to think about her career too much. Thinking about it unnerved him.

"Of course, there's this other wrinkle," she added, swimming up next to him. "Looks like one of the shooting victims is someone other than who or what he appears to be. So now I'm investigating the victim of an attempted murder, who is probably into something illegal—drugs, smuggling aliens— who knows? So is he a good guy or a bad guy?"

"I wouldn't have your job for all the rice in China," the doctor replied, shaking his head. "I don't know what you see in it. I swear I don't."

| ✶ |

Santos knocked this time, and the door flew open as if the broad shouldered woman inside intended to snatch it off its hinges. "Yeah?" she demanded. "Whatta you want? You another goddamn cop?"

"I'm trying to get in touch with Fernie." He took a half step forward.

The butch woman responded by stepping aggressively into the door frame, blocking it. From the smell of alcohol on her breath and the look in her eyes, he half expected her to try punching him in the face. "That little shit don't live here no more," she slurred, satisfaction shining through the blur of her speech. "Outta here! Gone!" She gestured smugly toward the street.

"Any idea where he went?" Santos asked, his voice level.

"No! Now get the fuck outta here." She started to slam

the door, but Santos was way ahead of her. His left shoulder rammed hard into the door, ripping it from the woman's hand, as the fingers and thumb of his right hand closed like steel bands around her larynx. She staggered heavily backward, clutching desperately at his hand as he shoved her inside. Unable to breathe, she collided with a chair and crashed hard into the wall, her face livid. He increased the pressure around her windpipe, enough to give her a sensation of impending death by suffocation. It was a feeling he intended she never forget.

"If you happen to see him, ask him to call me." He released her throat and let her slump to the floor, her doughy face still blue. "When you get your voice back."

Santos cruised by the phone where Fernie usually stood, but the kid was nowhere in sight. He parked near the alley behind the Mining Company and went into the bar. The back verandah looked out on the parking lot and the public phone by the street, the same street where he and Tony had been shot. He ordered a Corona and sat on a stool by the window, waiting. He'd been there for an hour before the boy's slender form finally materialized in the shadows under the arches of the parking structure across the street. The boy crossed the street toward the pay phone, a cheap tote bag slung over his skinny shoulder. Santos sighed at the sadness and predictability of it all, slid off the bar stool, and headed for the door.

"Fernie, you OK?"

The boy whipped around, on edge, startled at hearing his name spoken in the dark. His left eye had swollen nearly shut and a substantial bruise discolored his cheek.

Santos guessed his sister had a wicked right. "Why didn't you call me?"

The boy just shrugged.

"Come on, let's get something to eat." Santos took the bag

in hand and Fernie followed him to the Jeep, climbed in, and slumped in the seat, exhausted.

"My sister kicked me out."

"Looks more like she punched you out," Santos said. "She and I talked."

"You talked to her?"

"Not very long. Just enough for us to get to know each other."

Fernie rolled his eyes.

Santos pulled the Jeep out onto Ochoa. "Hungry?" Ochoa Street, scene of Tony's last night alive. Santos felt like he'd die for certain if he spent another minute there.

"I haven't eaten all day," Fernie answered. "I could use some food."

"I know a place that'll be open about another 30 minutes." Fernie had dressed well enough to get them into Jaxon's without someone tossing them out, he figured. "We can still make it if we step on it. After we eat I want to ask you about that cop who interviewed you."

"Which one?" the boy asked.

"What do you mean?" He suddenly recalled Fernie's sister had said something about another cop.

"The *vieja* came back, the tall one. With gray hair. She's the one that got my sister all mad and got me thrown out. Like she needed an excuse, *pinche puta de mierda.*"

Santos drove in silence for a few moments. He'd have to think how to handle this. Apparently Lessing hadn't given up yet. And he didn't want her ahead of him. "So what did you tell her?" he asked.

"Nothing, *hombre! Nada en absoluto.* My sister told her some shit about I went to Mexico to visit family or something."

Santos felt sure the boy had told him the truth, then wondered just how far Lessing would be willing to pursue this case, and why was she so interested in the first place?

"So where do I go after we finish talking?" Fernie asked.

"Back to my place, if that's OK with you." From Fernie's smile, Santos assumed it was.

CHAPTER FIFTEEN

Santos caught the I-10 off Sun Bowl, drove east through downtown, and turned north off the interstate at the Patriot Freeway. Passing Fort Bliss, he drove through the endless sprawl of subdivisions that had sprung up on the cheap land out in the desert valley. Where the freeway ran out, he slowed, watching carefully for the unmarked secondary roads he'd studied on the map.

The house faced a narrow stretch of gravel road, along with other houses and trailers spread out at long intervals in the chaparral for which the town had been named. Someone had crudely lettered L. DAVIS on a battered silver mailbox by the entrance to the driveway. The place was a simple clapboard affair, scoured to a light gray by years of sandstorms. It squatted behind a sagging wire fence, silently waiting for him. In the yard to the left of the house were two naked concrete strips that served as a primitive driveway. Davis, he supposed, worked days.

A few hundred yards down the road, out of sight of the houses, Santos swung the Jeep around, stopped, and studied the map. A utility road ran behind the row of houses. He turned in that direction, but drove past it twice before spotting it. A sandy trail, barely wide enough for a single vehicle, it snaked its way through clumps of greasewood and mesquite, dropping downward toward a depression in the desert floor. He parked the Jeep behind a low thicket of brush, picked a blue canvas bag with GOLD'S GYM printed on the side from the rear of the Jeep, and walked uphill toward the back of Davis's house. After a few minutes of hiking over rocks and sand, he stood at the rear perimeter of cheap wire fence.

Santos reached into the gym bag, pulled out a .25 caliber pistol with a silencer attached, scanned the yard, and let out a low whistle. Satisfied that there were no dogs, he stepped over the fence. Holding the pistol down by his side, he crossed the yard and tried the back door. It was securely locked. He removed an electronic pick from the bag, inserted the thin metal probe into the keyway, and pressed a button on the handle. The pick emitted a soft purring sound followed by a dull click. He removed his sunglasses before slipping into the warm stillness of the house.

Room by room, he performed a rapid reconnoiter of the dwelling: kitchen, hallway, bathroom, living room, a cramped bedroom adorned with a large red and black swastika. His survey complete, he returned to the kitchen, knelt, and planted a tiny transmitter under the table. He moved on to the living room, where he planted the next bug under the end table where Davis kept his phone. He then placed a specialized transmitter in the phone receiver and a final button mike attached to the iron bed frame.

Davis's stash of pornography lay under the bed. Santos extracted the stack of glossy magazines and glanced through it. Most of the pictures were of women who could pass for underage nymphets. The majority were shown taking dicks and dildos up the ass. Some were bound and gagged. One cover photo displayed a girl who looked 14 going on 40. A hefty, anonymous cock speared her vagina and another, equally thick, buried itself to the balls in her anus. Whatever Davis's actual sex life might amount to, it was clear his fantasies ran to bondage and butt fucking. The younger the girl, the better. Judging from the condition of the pages, Davis was a sloppy masturbator.

Santos placed the magazines in the position he'd found them and began a more thorough room-by-room search of the house. In a drawer in the bedroom he found a .45 caliber pistol and an extendable steel whip, a kind he knew could be ordered by mail. He held the whip up to the dim light. It looked like it had been used on someone. Kinky black hair had lodged in several of the coils along its length. When he flexed the steel, tiny flakes of dried blood dropped from between the openings. The drag queen in the park, he guessed. He dropped the weapon back into the drawer.

Davis had scribbled several numbers on the wall over the phone. Santos copied them quickly before slipping out the back door and hiking down to where his Jeep waited hidden in the brush. It was still several hours before he expected Davis to return home. But he decided not to push his luck.

Back in the Jeep he turned the receiver on and waited. A cicada warmed up in a bush nearby. Its initial clicking segued into a shrill metallic whine that shredded the rapidly warming air. Another insect replied from a distant thicket, then another. The foothills of the distant mountains appeared to shimmer. Santos unbuttoned his shirt, opened a jug of iced tea, and drank. The early afternoon spike, the hottest point of the day, had begun in earnest.

By the time the sun had progressed in its slow descent toward the mountaintops, the empty jug lay in the floor of the Jeep. Santos nudged it aimlessly with his boot. Pencil thin shadows of stunted trees inched silently across the sand. The cicadas had sung their brazen chorus and fallen silent. The black face of the receiver finally emitted a soft click, a tiny green dot began to blink, and the microcassette began to turn. Santos lifted the headphones to his ears. Footsteps echoed through the house, a refrigerator door opened and closed, followed by the pop of a pull top. The sounds faded as the subject moved out of the range of the device. Far from the microphone, a man urinated loudly into a toilet but didn't flush it.

Footsteps moved into the living room, where the sensitive mike picked up the sound of fingers tapping in numbers on the keypad of the phone. After three rings, a raspy male voice answered.

"Yeah?"

"Hey. Lyle here. The meeting still on for Wednesday?"

"Yeah. Good to go. Twenty-hundred hours. You're still coming, aren't ya?"

"Sure. You call the others?"

"Yeah. It's full dress, remember?"

"Absolutely."

As Santos watched, a phone number appeared on the receiver display. It was the number Davis had just dialed. Santos jotted it down.

"You there?" Davis asked.

"Yeah, I'm still here. Why?"

"Something the matter with the line there for a second. Reception out here sucks rocks."

Santos listened until the conversation ended, removed his headphones, unplugged them from the unit, and confirmed that it would continue to record when subsequent calls came through. Taking a roll of duct tape from his bag, he grabbed the small black box and climbed from the Jeep. He scanned the area for possible hiding places, deciding on a stunted clump of mesquite. He wedged the box securely between the lower branches and secured it with several wrappings of duct tape. He smiled grimly. A mesquite tree was a lot better place than a rectum for hiding a recording device.

He backed the Jeep out into the utility track and headed back to the main road, past Davis's house. The dusty dark-blue Camaro crouched in the driveway. Seeing it brought back flashes of imagery. The memory made him cringe like an animal shrinks from fire. Its bright yellow plate read WLFSKNS. He could stop the Jeep right here, walk into that house, and kill Davis on the spot. Or he could wait, identify his accomplices, and kill them all one by one. From the looks of things, he'd be avenging more than just Tony's murder.

Swallowing his hatred he pressed the accelerator and drove into the impending darkness. What difference would another week or two make? He'd already lost what mattered most. Besides, he'd secured the police report and the most important eyewitness would be asleep beside him in his bed tonight. He could afford to wait. Detective Lessing would never catch up.

| ✴ |

The intricate guitar work of Ottmar Liebert drifted softly through the stuffy apartment. Santos started to call for Fernie, but decided against it when he heard the boy's deep, steady breathing coming from the direction of the couch. He went to the kitchen and poured himself a tall glass of sweet iced tea. The heat had sapped him. The long wait in the desert and the drive back had left him feeling strangely disconnected. His skin felt hot and grainy, as if he'd been deep fried in oil and rolled in sand. He peeled off his shirt, dropped it on the kitchen floor, and headed for the shower. He stepped out of his jeans and underwear, leaving them in a heap on the bathroom tile. While he waited for the water to warm, he wrapped a towel around his waist and went back to check on Fernie. He'd fallen asleep on the couch, wrapped in Santos's bathrobe, but had kicked it off. Exposed, skinny like a child, he lay on his side, his knees partially drawn up. The thin, drooping skin of his scrotum cradled small, oval testicles, but his dense black bush framed a completely adult erection. Santos's eyes moved over the twin prows of his hipbones and up his flat stomach. Aware of the steady rise of his own sex, Santos pulled the robe back over the kid's nakedness, turned the air conditioner up a couple of clicks, and headed back toward the shower.

He stood under the burning stream of water, caressing himself. He ached for release. The bathroom door opened.

"Fernie?" He could barely see through the cloud of steam. The shower door slid open and the boy stepped in, still hard. Without a word, he knelt and took Santos's cock into his mouth. His lips began to move up and down the shaft. Santos shivered with pleasure.

"You're already close," Fernie said, stopping what he was doing and looking up. He stood and began to soap Santos's chest and arms, working his way slowly from part to part. "Rinse off." He turned Santos around in the spray. "Now do me," he said, handing Santos the soap.

Santos lathered his hands and spread the foam over Fernie's chest and back.

The boy moved closer, grasping both their cocks.

"*Ay, papacito,*" he whispered as Santos's fingers explored the cleft of his ass and gently entered him.

Santos let the stroking of Fernie's hand take him to the brink. "I'm going to cum," he said, pushing his fingers deeper into Fernie.

"*Ay, Dios!*" Fernie gasped.

Santos's climax was so intense he nearly collapsed.

He awoke in the small hours of the morning, disoriented in the dark, unable to guess how much time had passed since he'd fallen asleep. Fernie lay warm against him, his arm draped over Santos's chest, his moist, insistent firmness pressed against the side of Santos's thigh. He found the boy's smaller hand, took it in his, and fell back asleep.

CHAPTER SIXTEEN

The full moon flooded the desert with ghostly light. In the distance, the jagged, blackened teeth of the Organ Mountains cut into the night sky. Every hundred yards or so, the eyes of grazing jackrabbits caught the headlights of the Jeep and reflected back eerie, glowing points. When he turned onto the utility road that led to the back of Davis's place, he switched off his lights and drove under the moon.

Santos stopped near the thicket of mesquite where he'd hidden the small recorder, and still favoring his injured side, carefully climbed out into the thick shadows. The night air made his wounds ache. Something he couldn't see slithered away from his feet into a clump of dry brush. He switched on a flashlight to orient himself. On a branch in front of him sat a small, impassive brown owl, its huge yellow eyes staring into his. "Hello there," he whispered to it. "You hunting too?" The bird blinked, turned its head to catch some sound Santos couldn't hear, and flew silently away.

Santos retrieved the recording device and sat for a long while with it in his lap. The tape told him everything he could have hoped for. Laying the recorder on the seat beside him, he started the Jeep and headed back toward the gravel road that led past Davis's house. A police black-and-white sat parked behind the blue Camaro. Santos didn't slow as he passed. He already knew the identity of its driver.

|☀|

Ron Schneider sat on the hood of his pickup and watched the road. He hated doing guard duty on the perimeter, but J.T. had been adamant about the arrangements. The water-worn gravel in the dry wash crunched under his boots as he slid down to stretch his legs. He lit a cigarette. J.T. would not have approved. J.T. maintained that the glow of a cigarette could betray the position of a sentry. Sometimes J.T. took shit way too seriously, some hang-up left over from The 'Nam, Ron supposed. Fuck J.T. anyway. He inhaled deeply and then exhaled a defiant plume into the night air.

Ron took another pull from his cigarette and paused. Out here in BFE, nearly all the roads were gravel. Cars couldn't move quietly over the stuff. He heard one now, headed toward his post. He raised a pair of night-scope binoculars in time to see Lyle's blue Camaro pass in the dark. Neal Pearson, one of the recruits to be inducted tonight, sat on the passenger side. Ron spat between his teeth. He sensed a softness about Pearson, a vulnerability he despised.

Ron ground the remnant of his cigarette under the heel of his boot and started to hop back up on the hood of his truck when he heard a second vehicle approaching. He peered through the binoculars. A Jeep this time. Ed Farris drove a Jeep, but Ed had already taken up his position at the church. So it couldn't be his. Ron watched as the Jeep passed, driving with its lights off. He read off the plate number under his breath, repeating it a couple of times. The driver, a tall, mus-cular man, wore a dark baseball cap and dark clothing. Ron switched on his portable radio.

"Yeah Ron, what's up?" Farris asked

"Heads up, man. Some guy in a Jeep just passed here, following Lyle. With his lights off, OK?"

"Sure it's not one of our guys just clowning around?"

Farris's stupidity made Ron want to scream. "Why the hell would one of our guys be driving around out here with his lights off, dumb-fuck?"

"Chill out, will you? Hang on a minute." The handset spluttered faintly with background static. Ron waited for what seemed like eternity before Ed spoke again. "Ron?"

"Yeah, what?"

"J.T. says to just watch and see if the guy comes back out. Don't approach him. You get a look at his plates?"

"Yeah, I got 'em."

"Great. J.T. thinks it might be a federal agent. Leave him alone, OK?" Ed sounded breathless. "We've got a right to assemble. Says so in the Constitution. So just leave him alone, OK?"

"Yeah, Eddy. I under-fucking-stand fucking English. I'm leaving him alone."

Ron clicked off the handset in exasperation "Dipshits," he muttered. For a movement that represented the future of America, they sure had some fuck-ups for members. If it were up to him, they'd go find this guy right now and take him out. In a mood somewhere between worried and bored, he repositioned himself on the hood of the truck and lit another smoke.

| ☆ |

The darkness and the thin trail of dust raised by the Camaro's tires allowed the Jeep to follow undetected by the Camaro's occupants. Santos tailed the car over a ridge, watched it descend, and saw its brake lights flash as it turned off into a church parking lot. He stopped the Jeep, put it into reverse, and backed it over the ridge, out of the line of sight.

He'd seen the entrance to a ranch a few hundred feet back. Backing up slowly, he managed to spot it. The spaced pipes of the cattle guard rattled loudly as he drove down the narrow track. Weeds had grown in the ruts. The road probably led to an abandoned ranch house or some facility that saw very little use. He pulled the Jeep off into an area of hardened, rocky ground, positioned it behind a clump of stunted trees, and cut the engine. Shouldering a light backpack, he slid down from the seat. The silence of the night enfolded him.

Steep-sided gullies with treacherously unstable edges, clumps of spiny cactus, and dwarf trees studded with thorns that were inches long slowed his progress to a crawl. After 20 minutes of threading his way cautiously around prickly natural obstacles, he crouched in the shadow of a stand of slender ocotillo, raised his binoculars, and scanned the surroundings of the concrete block church. At the edge of the parking area a dark figure sat hunkered down in a Jeep. Its doors were open to admit the night air. When the man shifted, Santos could make out an assault rifle resting across his legs. To see inside the building, he would need to move down another hundred feet of hillside. Easing along crabwise, he continued his descent.

He stopped in the mouth of a shallow draw, his head below the line of sight of anyone who might approach from either side. He raised his binoculars. From this new vantage point, he could see in through a window. A stocky man in gray battle dress—gold braids and all—stood behind a podium, flanked on either side by two men in tan uniforms. Three men—two older, the other just a kid—stood at rigid attention facing the speaker. Behind them, an audience of men, women, and children sat on folding chairs, listening raptly to the heavy man in gray.

Santos extracted a slender microphone and a small dish antenna from the backpack, assembled the unit, and aimed the device toward the window. He could catch enough of the speaker's diatribe to understand that the congregation had gathered for an initiation ceremony, an induction of new troops in the war to save America. He instantly recognized the speaker's raspy voice from the recordings of Lyle's phone conversations: J.T. Mallory, the cop who had signed the falsified police report, and, very likely, Tony's death warrant.

Santos observed Mallory for long minutes, watching the changing contortions of his face. His voice came through the earpiece sporadically as the dish captured and then lost it again. Santos was reminded of old film clips of Hitler haranguing the masses, his face bloated with certainty, spewing out spit and hatred.

Santos watched a while longer, surprised by his lack of emotion.

Before the ceremony ended, Santos stowed the microphone and his binoculars, and headed back up the hill. He'd take them down, one by one. He'd promised Tony that much. But he'd save Mallory for last.

A stab in the calf from a dark clump of cactus reminded him to stay focused on the path.

At any rate, given the remoteness of the church, entering it without detection would be simplicity itself. As he threaded his way back over loose rocks, intent on avoiding the hostile vegetation, he let his mind run through his options.

| ✶ |

When she entered the office the next morning, there was a yellow fax on top of her stack of paperwork. Lessing picked it up and read it. The FBI computers had not been able to find a clear match with Santos's photo. The form suggested she submit fingerprints and gave a toll-free number to call if she had further questions.

She had plenty of questions, but none that an 800 number would be likely to answer. Besides, just how and under what authority could she obtain a set of Santos's fingerprints? Especially when she lacked probable cause to be investigating him in the first place.

CHAPTER SEVENTEEN

By 9:27 A.M. the temperature had already climbed to 88 degrees. Santos noted it as he drove by the Bank of America on the way to the storage facility where he had rented a space. He passed the office, stopped at the gated entrance, and tapped his code in on the keypad. He waited for the sliding iron gate to creak open.

A shower of fresh dust drifted from the storage compartment door as it rolled upward. He walked into the hot, stale air of the enclosure. Several of the crates leaked a faint smell of Cosmoline. With a crowbar he opened one of the crates. He removed an antipersonnel mine from the crate and placed it in the canvas gym bag. From the top of another box, he picked up a nail gun and blew away its reddish coating of dust. He closed the door, padlocked it, and tossed the bag and nail gun into the back of the Jeep.

Santos stopped for breakfast at the Village Inn up the street from the storage facility and perused the El Paso and Juárez newspapers while he worked his way through a short stack, a side order of sausage, and four cups of coffee. He skipped the sports section, but glanced through the society pages of the Mexican paper, where, as always, the toothy unmarried girls of rich families were copiously photographed.

Even here girls were being pimped, but discreetly and in the best of taste. Gregorio referred to the *La Sociedad* section as "the do-my-daughter pages."

After breakfast, Santos stopped by a cavernous home improvement store where he bought a box of .22 caliber blanks and spool of thin wire. In the Jeep, he made a final inventory of the contents of the gym bag and his collection of tools before heading toward the freeway that would take him over the Franklin mountains and out to Chaparral, New Mexico. Quicksilver heat already shimmered up from the asphalt. El Paso's three weeks of spring had burned off into summer a week early.

| * |

Lyle Davis wheeled the Camaro into the driveway, jolted to a halt, and yanked up on the emergency brake. Eager to escape the car's inadequate air conditioning, he pushed the door open, only to be engulfed by a stifling blast of hot air as he hauled his frame up out of the bucket seat. The inside of the house probably wouldn't be that much better, he figured, but at least a 12-pack of cold ones awaited him in the fridge.

"Christ on a crutch! How much hotter can this shit get?" he complained to no one in particular. The reality was that this shit could and would get a lot hotter. Summer had barely started. He wore a cowboy shirt with the sleeves cut out at the shoulders. Perspiration plastered the thin material to the contours of his back. He started peeling the shirt off as he crossed the yard. Why hadn't he thought to do that before now? Goddamn it was hot! He unlocked the door, jerked it open, and stepped into the living room. Compared to the glare outside, the inside of the house seemed pitch black.

The jolt of the stun gun, hitting him below the base of his

skull, dropped him straight to the floor, arms and legs in helpless spasm. He felt a hot stream of piss run down his leg. Someone slammed the door behind him, grabbed him by the hair and dragged him, still twitching, into the middle of the living room. He willed himself to hit, kick, but his limbs would not obey. He tried to shout, but couldn't manage anything louder than a faint croak.

He could make out a shadowy figure standing over him— a tall, muscular man. The man pressed a squarish metal object hard against Davis's hand and a trigger clicked. Only then did Davis realize what the object was. He heard the blanks explode, and felt a pair of nails drive through his flesh and into the floor. A gurgling scream formed in his throat. Davis watched in horror as the man moved to his left side, pinned his still-jittering arm to the floor, and used the gun to drive two thick nails through that hand, too. Strong fingers then pinched a fold of skin inside his arm. An explosion nailed it to the worn linoleum. The figure crossed back to his other side and repeated the process.

Davis thought he felt his strength coming back a little and attempted a kick. The dark figure blocked it effortlessly. And this time the stun gun caught him under the right knee cap, slamming a bolt of fire up the bone of his leg, through his ass, and into his back. Davis's eyes had adjusted to the dim light in the house, and he could see his assailant more clearly now. The man held a knife, the blade curved in an evil smile. The razor edge winked at Davis in the watery light. A thin wail escaped Davis's throat while his legs quivered like a spastic marionette. The knife cut away Davis's pants and underwear in long, smooth strokes, and the man ripped the cloth away, exposing him completely.

"No-o-o!" Davis screamed. Four more explosions nailed his feet to the floor, spiking him through his shoes. Davis sobbed. Terrified, he begged the man to stop. The same strong fingers seized a generous pinch of his scrotum, stretched it taut, and neatly drove two nails through it. The pain made his stomach flip. He turned his head and spewed bile across the floor, mixing it with the blood pooling under his arm.

"Have you figured out who I am?" The figure spoke for the first time, his voice as measured and full of calm as Davis's mind was full of fear. "Probably not thinking too clearly, huh?"

Davis sobbed and shook his head.

"I'm one of the faggots you and your buddies shot for sport in front of the Old Plantation. Maybe you remember that." The man paused long enough for this to sink into Davis's reeling brain. "You killed my lover. He was just a kid." The man paused, examining his handiwork before looking back into Davis's eyes. "Obviously you should have killed me instead, you worthless, stupid fuck." The man stood. "You shit-eating waste of life. If I could kill you a thousand times, I would. But I can't, so I guess this once will have to do."

The man walked out of Davis's sight. In a moment he returned, holding a gallon can of gasoline in one hand and one of Davis's beers in the other. He held the red gas can up high so Davis could see it. "In another few seconds, I'm going to set this shitty rathole you live in on fire." The man took a long pull off the beer. "All you have to do to save yourself is get up and run." With that, the man splattered gasoline across the couch, then poured it in a broad arc on the floor around Davis's supine body.

Fumes began to sear Davis's throat. "Goddamn you," he spit as he attempted to raise a hand. The pain brought bile back into his throat.

The man tossed the beer can casually into a corner, tore a page from the phone book on the table by the couch, and carefully rolled it into a taper. He touched a lighter to it and held it aloft momentarily for Davis's inspection. Then he dropped the flame into a corner. The gasoline ignited with a roar. Davis lurched up with a shriek, the soaring flames reflected in his dilated pupils. "Last stop before hell, Lyle!" the man called from behind him as he strode from the room.

Santos stepped into the bedroom, closed the door, and jammed it shut. He dropped from the window to the driveway with a dull thud. He looked around, saw no one. The cooling engine of Davis's car still emitted a series of gentle clicks and pings. The sun had just dropped below the tops of the distant purple peaks. He covered the backyard at a trot. From inside the burning house he could hear Davis's muffled screams.

]✱[

On the trip out, Jen drove while Chuy sweated over the map and the air conditioning labored. An impenetrable cloud of dust rose behind the car. Far ahead of them, two fire trucks blocked the road. Off-road, she spotted an MP vehicle sitting high on its wheels next to a state trooper's car. Chaparral must lie within the boundary of Fort Bliss military reservation, she guessed.

"Sorry to get you officers out here in this ungodly heat."

Lessing made the taller of the two MPs for a good 6 foot 2, two hundred forty pounds and not an ounce of fat. He reminded her of her father. Fit, hair cropped to the skull, career army from a mile away. She and Chuy walked behind him through the thickening heat. Jen realized she'd had no idea how hot it got down here in the valley.

The medical examiner lumbered toward them, mopping his pink forehead with a handkerchief, and introduced himself. "This is the damnedest crime scene I've ever come across, folks, and I've seen a few, even in Alamogordo." He removed his tie and opened his shirt. Damp gray chest hair sprouted from under his collar. The sight of it made Jen glad not to be a man, particularly on a day like today. She wondered how much longer it would be before the guy heatstroked.

Everything but the back wall of the house and part of the kitchen doorway had burned to the ground. The kitchen sink stood in midair, supported on its pipes. A photographer and his assistant worked the charred ruins, finding little to take pictures of. Davis's body, contracted in the grotesque rictus of those who die by fire, lay on its back just inside what remained of the kitchen doorway. Fragments of overcooked flesh lay strewn around the body.

Lessing held her hand over her nose and mouth; the stench from Davis's carcass was so strong she could taste it. As they approached, a cloud of fat green blowflies rose from the feast, buzzing in protest.

"Well, first off, the skin of his balls is missing," the M.E. began. "Looks like it was avulsed. Pulled off, in other words. Testicles hanging by the spermatic cords. Hard to tell from the shape he's in, but looks like some skin was ripped off his arms, too, not burned away. The M.E. scooped sweat from his forehead and slung it away. "Possibly by the blast, but possibly not." He squatted by the corpse and pointed with his ball-point pen. "There's a couple of nails in his feet."

Lessing willed herself to bend close enough to see clearly. The blackened toes curled like claws around the soles of the burned shoes.

"But the nails sure as shit didn't do all this." With a sweep of his arm, the sweating man indicated the charred flesh sprayed across the floor. "Sergeant Franks here has determined he was hit by some kind of mine."

"Claymore," Franks interjected. "Antipersonnel mine that

blows out horizontally. Looks like he came through the door-way here." The burly sergeant pointed to the space between the burned-out remnants of the walls. "Running from the fire, from the looks of it. Hit a trip wire. Probably strung low across the door. The claymore detonated from the rear wall of the kitchen. Here, about eight feet away from him. Eviscerated him. Blew his guts all over the kitchen. You can see how they're blown back away from him. Then the fire caught up with him and finished him off."

Jen looked over at Chuy. Her partner's brick-colored mestizo face had gone a particularly nasty shade of ivy. Small beads of sweat sparkled on his upper lip. The group stood silently, hands over their mouths, taking in the carnage. Jen watched as her partner swallowed what must have been some of that morning's breakfast.

"There's a gun in the glove box of the car, along with the guy's registration," the M.E. offered.

"Be sure we get a report on the ballistics," Jen said, glad for any reason to put some distance between herself and the charred remains. The M.E. was right, she thought. This was the goddamnedest crime scene she'd ever seen, and she'd come from a bigger place than Alamogordo.

The front tires of the Camaro had melted in the heat, and much of the bubbled-up paint had burned away. But the car itself, having been upwind of the blaze, hadn't caught fire. Jen walked slowly around it a couple of times before she noticed the curious tags. She fished her notebook from her purse.

"Jesus, Mary, and Joseph. I'll never live long enough to get *that* out of my head," Chuy remarked as he drove them back to the freeway. "I've gotta get out of this business. I'm getting too old for this crap."

"Yeah," Jen agreed, grimacing. "That was pretty extreme. And I doubt if the cleaners can get the smell out of these clothes. May have to just throw them away."

The late afternoon heat smothered the desert like a dusty shroud. A television news van came toward them in its own cloud of dust, headed out to the crime scene. "News at 11," Chuy said.

"What are they going to *show?*" Jen asked. "There's nothing left they could put on TV."

Jen was itching to run the Camaro plates, but they had no computer terminal in the car. She contented herself with staring at the letters jotted in her notebook. Obviously a vanity plate of some kind. All consonants. She mentally supplied vowels until she came up with "wolf skins." Whatever that meant. If there were still any wolves in New Mexico, which seemed unlikely, they'd be living hundreds of miles to the north. So what else could it mean? A club of some kind? What if "skins" referred to skinheads? The car was registered to one Lyle Davis, the same name as on the mailbox by the road. But was the DOA Lyle Davis? If so, who had killed him? And why?

Chuy's theory was that the killing amounted to nothing more than a particularly grisly drug hit. When you hear hoofbeats, look for horses, not zebras, he'd reminded her. And he was probably right. After all, someone had torched that corrupt border patrol guy and his wife up in Cloudcroft back during the winter.

But a couple of things kept bothering Jen. If Davis had been dealing enough drugs to make him worth killing, where was the money? The guy had been living in a shit-hole out in the middle of nowhere and driving a piece of crap.

And the similarity between this case and the Cloudcroft killings might be more apparent than real. The killing of the border patrolman and his wife was businesslike, impersonal, the fire meant to destroy evidence. This killing was as personal as it got. The guy back there had been meant to go down bad. Somebody had hated his guts enough to spray them all over his kitchen. Someone had planned his death in meticulous detail.

Drug hits were always designed to leave a message. But could this death have been intended to leave a message that had nothing to do with the drug trade? If so, for whom? Within a few days they'd have the ballistics back. Dental forensics for a firm identification. DMV and phone records. A criminal background check. Then they'd have something to go on.

]✶[

Santos parked off the abandoned ranch road again, and made his way slowly down the hillside, his progress through the blasted vegetation and sunburned rocks covered by the fading light. To his left a cactus wren cocked its head inquisitively, its tail jerking up and down. Over the hill a butcher bird croaked. How did they live out here in this inferno? The wren trilled once and flew a surreptitious zigzag path down the slope, staying close to the ground.

He unshouldered his pack and shrugged his aching back. It had been a long day. Feeling slightly better, he assumed the load once more and headed downhill toward the church. Only a couple of hours of daylight remained.

CHAPTER EIGHTEEN

There were many things Fernie did not know, but there were several that he did. For one, Santos held no regular job, yet never seemed short of money. He also kept irregular hours, sometimes sleeping through much of the day and disappearing at night, sometimes staying out all day and coming home well after dark. At first Fernie thought that his benefactor might be selling drugs, but he quickly discarded that idea. Santos rarely turned on his cell phone and didn't even own a beeper. Besides, there wasn't the continuous to and fro of people that went with retailing drugs. And they lived in an apartment high above the city, hardly a convenient place for a dealer.

He and Santos went out several times a week, usually to eat or watch a movie. But Santos never visited family or friends. In fact, Santos seemed to have no friends. And apart from junk advertising and some catalogs sent to former residents, no mail came to the apartment.

After their first sex together in the shower, Fernie shared Santos's bed continuously, wanting the tenderness even more than the pleasuring. Though no promises had been made, he felt sure that Santos had no other sexual partners. But Santos's long term intentions remained unclear.

Fernie knew that Santos, who tossed and sometimes cried out in his sleep, still missed the boy who had been killed. Then, two days ago, Santos had asked him if he wanted them to be together, to go away somewhere, far away. Soon. And Fernie cried, partly because he would leave the places he knew, but mostly because he had no other choices. It was Santos or the street. Knowing that Santos might be keeping him out of a sense of charity just made his situation that much harder.

Yesterday morning they'd driven to Las Cruces, sold the Jeep for cash, and taken a cab around to various used car lots. Within a couple of hours, they'd found a used Pathfinder, fully loaded. Santos paid for it in cash. And that night, they'd packed their belongings in the Pathfinder and left. When Fernie asked, Santos told him the furniture had been rented. The company, Santos assured him, would come by later and pick it up.

At the moment, Santos slept, his hard biceps enfolding Fernie's undeveloped chest, and Fernie, more excited than afraid about the turn of events, resolved to live in the moment and let things unfold without too much questioning. Even adrift like this, living in a hotel, with Santos he felt safe.

All told, it had taken Santos less than 24 hours to wrap up his affairs.

|＊|

J.T. Mallory leaned back in the well-worn recliner and popped the tab on another Bud. The beer wasn't making his headache any better, but at this point he didn't care. Right now he figured the headache to be the least of his worries. Hoping to get lucky, he'd run a tag trace on the Jeep that Ron Schneider had spotted out in the desert. It had been registered to some Jesús Something-or-other. Mallory guessed there were only about a billion or two taco benders named Jesús. The mailing address turned out to be some P.O. box, never rented to anyone named Goncalva. And the permanent address? A vacant lot in J-town. Right now, their man was as much of a phantom as his fake addresses.

J.T. figured Lyle's place as a nonstarter as far as "Jesús" was concerned. The fire had burned up fingerprints, and the desert wind had sifted sand into whatever footprints or tire tracks existed. On the other hand, only God knew what it would disclose to investigators about Lyle. The identity of the group could be blown wide open.

Mallory figured the Jeep, if he bothered to look for it, would be out of state by now, probably abandoned or sold, already with new tags. Whatever his background, the guy who'd done Lyle knew his shit. Mallory had seen nothing to equal it in calculation and brutality since a Spec Ops interrogator he'd worked for in 'Nam had heated a screwdriver red-hot and stuck it up some slant's dick. It got the guy to talking, too, in between screams. That's what they should have done with their mystery man, then popped a cap in his ass, whoever the fuck he was, the very night they'd spotted him. Now, here J.T. sat. Screwed. A day late, a dollar short, and at the wrong address, his daddy would have said. At least the old man hadn't lived to see this, he thought. He'd been in charge, and bungled his command. Maybe time had caught up with him. Sooner or later it did with everyone.

Worse yet, he could come up with no credible perp. No one but a few boys dressed as girls had gone to the funeral of the nigger they'd hit. Not even the fag's own family showed up. He knew 'cause he'd staked it out. And that fag boy and his fudge-packing butt buddy? Sissy-boy was dead. Shot to shit. And the other guy was just another weightlifting homo, flexing his muscles so he could feel like a man. Nothing to worry about there. But who else?

Maybe Lyle had pissed off the wrong guy. Maybe Lyle was porking the girlfriend of some special forces type out on the base. That, at least, would explain the calculation and professionalism of the way Lyle had gone down. And that would have been about Lyle's speed, he knew from previous experience. Lyle always acted out his silent bad-ass role, tougher than tough, overestimating his abilities. Lyle, always in over his head. In six feet of dirt over his head now. Mallory sighed in resignation. Davis had just been young, that's all.

Now this shit was turning up a lot of loose ends. He'd watch the news again tonight, see if the cops had uncovered anything else. Of course if it was something good, the cops wouldn't be yapping it to the media. Right now he couldn't seem to be too interested, poking around at the station. But one thing he knew for sure: Headquarters would expect him to clean up the mess, even if it meant silencing some people.

| ✻ |

"This'll make you cream," Chuy said, handing Jen the ballistics report. "Real police work. Just what you moved down here for."

"OK, let's see just how wet you can get me, Chuy. Maybe you're even more of an animal than I thought." She took a slow bite from her sandwich while she read, then chewed while she reread the ballistics sheet. "The test bullets from the gun in Davis's glove compartment are a match for that shooting in front of the gay bar last month," she announced. She swallowed and laid the sandwich aside. "That guy Davis was one of the shooters."

"Not necessarily," Acevedo said. "Davis could have

picked that gun up somewhere. He coulda bought it hot. Got himself a bargain. You know guns get around."

"That business out in the desert was a revenge killing, Chuy."

"By who? The boyfriend?" Chuy helped himself to a cup of coffee from Jen's thermos. "That guy got pretty shot up. Besides, that thing in Chaparral had 'pro' written all over it. I'm telling you, that guy Davis, there's no telling what he got himself involved in. Smuggling drugs, wetbacks, you name it. Hell, smuggling goddamn parrots, even! But drugs, most likely." He took a swig of coffee and winced.

Jen smiled. He deserved to burn his mouth on purloined coffee.

"And no family ever came forward on either of those guys who got shot. Not that *I* saw. So how does that make it revenge?"

"Taking Davis out like that was pretty extreme, even by drug-dealer standards," she countered. "And if Davis was all up to his neck in drugs or whatever, where's his money? Guy's living in a shack." But Acevedo had a point. No family had come forward after the kid's shooting. De La O had handled all the arrangements himself. So if killing Davis had really been revenge for the boy's murder, who did that leave as a suspect? Just Santos De La O.

"I don't know," Chuy said. "The revenge thing seems pretty farfetched to me. But I've seen dealers do some pretty extreme shit. You fuck with those guys, they'll microwave your mother and blow her ashes up your ass." Chuy blew on the coffee. Incredible how hot the stuff could stay in a thermos. "Hell, maybe that De La Homo guy did this. Interview him again. Or maybe there's another explanation for the killing. I mean, just because Davis shoots some fag...gay guy, whatever, it doesn't mean that was the *only* thing he was mixed up in."

Chuy's scenario, Jen had to admit, contained a real possibility. Lyle Davis had been a bad man. Probably bad enough to have had many enemies. Was she seeing a connection where none existed? Could she be scapegoating De La O? Did she suspect him because he was gay? She rejected that possibility; she didn't think that way. Or did she? Besides, she had no proof, absolutely none, that De La O had offed Davis. Besides, where would De La O get an antipersonnel mine? "Speaking of Mr. De La O, it just so happens, inconveniently for us, that the file on that case has gone missing. Not signed out, just disappeared." Jen leveled her gaze at her partner and held it, waiting for a reaction. Could he have taken it? Could he be covering up for someone who had? But Chuy just sat on the edge of her desk, drinking stolen coffee, unperturbed.

"Hell, there's a lot of paperwork goes missing around here, Jen. Some of it by accident," he added, chuckling. "Papers get stuck in the wrong file. Slide down behind drawers. Some of it probably just plain gets thrown out by the cleaning people."

"Yeah, but I've got a feeling about this case." Listening to herself made Jen flinch. Cops with hunches were a cliché, she knew. And spectacular homicides were not, in fact, rare here or across the border, although the ones across the border were sometimes more bizarre and ran to bigger numbers. Like dozens of dead girls turning up in vacant lots.

Chuy shrugged and ambled back to his desk. The springs of his swivel chair complained as he lowered his weight. He went back to typing a report.

Jen resumed her lunch. The bread of her sandwich had gone dry at the edges. The coroner's report on Davis would be out tomorrow or the next day. Maybe it would tell them something.

]★[

Gregorio looked across the table at his liaison, Don Carlos. For once he hadn't ordered anything to eat. The news had stunned even him. "Just so you know, all right?" the messenger said.

"Yeah, sure," Gregorio replied. "*No hay problema.*" He felt like he'd gone pale. He wondered if it showed.

"*Muy bien,*" the other replied, rising to leave. "*Cuídate, pues.*"

Yes, Gregorio thought, *take care of myself. Good advice. That is exactly what I intend to do.*

They'd decided to use the rockets and dispose of Santos. To burn the trail of evidence, Gregorio supposed. A cold, calculated business decision. Just like them, *desalmadamente.* He searched his mind for the word in English. Yes, of course, "heartless." Cold calculation, after all, was the only way to stay alive in this business. It came as no surprise if you thought about it. Rightly considered, one could concede that the plan contained a certain elegant logic.

"*Pues, ni modo,*" he muttered. He'd developed a certain affection for De La O, and certainly respect for his competence. He'd never had to explain the "how" to Santos. He shrugged it off. The question now was how much time remained until the bosses decided to punch *his* ticket? He tossed some money on the table to cover the drinks and left, his mind whirling with plans. His command of English had improved enormously over the past year. A good thing, too, because he'd need it soon.

CHAPTER NINETEEN

The battered Ford pickup rattled to a stop in front of the burned out ruin that had been Lyle Davis's house. The dust the truck had raised caught up with it and slowly began to settle onto its oxidized red paint. The smell of fire and a hint of something worse drifted into the open window along with the dust. Neal Pearson sat motionless, ignoring the heat and drifting dirt, just looking out at it all. Eventually he opened the door and got out.

A long strip of yellow tape ran from the fence, across the front gate, and back to the fence. Neal first tried tearing out a piece of it, but couldn't. Furious, he ripped it all off the fence, wadded it into a big sticky ball, and threw it into the road. What remained of the floor looked like it might collapse if stepped on, so he walked around the perimeter. Toward the rear, where the back door jamb and portions of wall still survived, the smell of death rose powerfully to greet him. A long column of ants moved across the charred linoleum toward a small clump of something, swarmed over it, making it look fuzzy, and scurried back into the ranks, carrying it off one tiny bite at a time. Neal ran heaving to the side of the yard, bent over, and sprayed his breakfast onto the sand for the ants to find. He wiped his mouth and stood for a while, surveying what little remained of Lyle's place. Then he turned and walked dejectedly back toward the road. On the news, with the reporter in the foreground, it had somehow looked like more. In fact, next to nothing remained of Lyle Davis or his house.

The dull red pickup sped away, its rear wheels flinging up angry rooster tails of rocks and dust as the driver popped the clutch and stomped on the gas. Jen waited for the truck to disappear before rising, knees protesting, from behind the stunted thicket across the road. In spite of the strongest sunscreen she'd been able to find, the back of her neck felt ready to blister. She decided to call it a day. A productive day, too, she thought, hefting the powerful telephoto lens. She trusted Fred would never notice the temporary loss of his beloved toy. He hadn't taken his camera out of the closet since their trip down to Port Aransas to snap whooping cranes. Jen rewound the film, opened the back, and dropped the spool out into the palm of her hand.

She decided having the film commercially processed would be the smart thing to do, rather than turning it over to the police lab. After all, the appearance of a police officer driving a squad car in surveillance photos might raise unwanted speculation within the porous department. Maybe if he'd been wearing civilian clothes and driving his own car, she might not have recognized him as quickly. But J.T. Mallory in uniform was just plain impossible to miss. There would be time enough tomorrow to run a trace on the pickup's plates and catch up with the kid driving the truck. Probably just a friend of the deceased, trying to come to grips. But why would Mallory be interested enough to drive all the way out here? And how would he even have known where to find it? The roads that crisscrossed the small desert town were anything but clear.

She laid the camera carefully in the front seat, slid in next to it, and fastened her seat belt. She had an idea. Why didn't she think of it before? Maybe the heat had started to cook her brain. Maybe walking around in a permanent stupor went with living in the desert. There certainly seemed to be a lot of stupor going around.

| ✷ |

Ron Schneider tossed his cigarette on the ground and rubbed it out with the heel of his boot. Schneider, raised on a New Mexico ranch, accepted repetitive, mindless chores without question. Like cleaning the auditorium of the church every Saturday. Just part of the flow of life. Of course, today he'd be cleaning it with ass-licker Ed. That would make the project "a learning experience." Although Schneider didn't mind routine, he hated wasting time, which he happened to be doing at the moment. "Come on, will ya?"

Farris still sat in his Jeep, scarfing down some tacos-to-go crap he'd bought back where the freeway petered out. Sauce oozed from the folds of the tortilla concoction and dripped on his dingy T-shirt. Farris continued to chew, glaring at Schneider with dumb annoyance.

"Quit stuffin' your face and let's get started!" Schneider yelled.

"*What* is the fucking hurry?" Farris shot back. "A guy can't even eat with you around."

Schneider dropped brooms, mops, a bucket with a wringer, and a bundle of rags by the door. He felt in his pocket, discovered that Farris had the door key, and sighed. He could spend the morning screaming at the fat drag-ass pigging out in the Jeep, or he could get mellow and get through it as best he could. The second option would give him time for another smoke. Shielding his match with one hand, he lit up and walked around to the shady side of the church. The restless air softly banged a metal window frame. Schneider jumped.

He'd been on edge ever since that shit had gone down with Lyle. He took a deep breath and willed himself to relax. Someone was always forgetting to close the damn windows. People out here either took security too lightly or got freaked out about nothing. He'd close it once Farris Wheel got his hooves out of the trough and unlocked the door. For the moment, he leaned back against the wall to enjoy the last lingering coolness of the morning. When he finally heard the door of Farris's Jeep slam shut, he flipped the stump of his cigarette into the sand and headed back toward the front door. "Toss me the keys," he called.

Farris dug them out, and pitched them over.

Schneider took them out of the air with the kind of clean, casual catch he imagined a klutz like Farris would envy. He unlocked and opened the door. Since Wednesday night, a miniature sand dune had drifted against it. He steered the mop bucket with his foot, but the small rubber wheels jammed against the sill.

"Move it, will ya?" ordered Farris. "It's gettin' hot out here."

Schneider could almost feel Farris's sweating bulk heaving itself up the narrow concrete walk behind him. He gave the bumper of the bucket a brisk kick to propel it over the sill. It jumped the sill, but still seemed snagged on something. Farris stood behind him now, crowding him. Schneider swore under his breath, planted a boot against the bucket, and gave it a shove.

Whatever had impeded the bucket suddenly wasn't there anymore. From the interior of the building something metallic clicked. A realization too terrible for words bubbled to the surface of Schneider's mind. Time froze.

Schneider hurled himself to his left and felt himself falling as if suspended in clear, viscous syrup. The searing light of a hundred suns ripped through the doorway. A sharpened fist punched him in the thigh. The concrete blocks in the wall in front of him clicked past his eyes in slow motion—click...click...click, one after another. Pungent smoke boiled in the air around him. His shoulder slammed into the ground and he felt his head bounce from the impact. Feeling his head whack the ground seemed to turn time back to normal speed.

He lay quietly for a moment, stunned, not sure if he was still alive. He attempted an inventory. He could breathe. Good. His hands clenched into fists when his brain commanded them to. His hands moved over his chest, his belly, his dick and balls. He could not look down yet, could not yet will himself to see what might be gone. He moved his left leg gingerly, then his right. Pain. Something wrong. He forced himself to sit up. Blood seeped from the ripped fabric of his jeans. Cautiously, he peeled back the warm, sticky denim. One of the hinges and some jagged daggers of wood from the door jamb protruded from the muscle of his thigh.

A sound like a baby gurgling broke his contemplation of his leg. He turned and saw Farris through the swirling dust and smoke. He'd forgotten all about him.

Farris, his bloody face the very picture of concentration, knelt while he carefully scooped his intestines up off the ground. He attempted to stand. A slippery handful of guts escaped his grasp, wriggling through his fingers. He made a grab for the loops of bowel, and missed. The sudden motion upset his balance and he tumbled over backward into the dirt.

Schneider giggled hysterically. Even in a situation like this, Farris looked and acted more like a cartoon than a person.

The image of Farris wallowing around on the ground while attempting to scoop up his insides was the last thing

Schneider remembered before coming to in the back of a jolting ambulance.

] * [

Santos awoke in a pool of sweat. The weather wasn't the only thing heating up. The explosion at the church had made the news. The cops were under real pressure to solve this one. Newscasters were already beginning to draw comparisons to the burning of churches in the South, and the city's religious leaders, Catholic, Protestant, and Jewish, white, black, and Hispanic, had rallied downtown in front of police headquarters, demanding to know what monster had set off a bomb in a House of God.

The rising tide of interest would bring the police investigation into sharper focus, and probably bring in federal agents since explosives were clearly involved. Santos understood that going after Mallory now would entail an even greater risk of discovery because, unless he was dense beyond belief, the cop would certainly have guessed that he was next on the list. Whatever Santos felt toward the motherfucker, assuming his opponent was stupid would be a major tactical mistake.

Santos lay in bed and pondered his options. He'd always known there would come a time to cut and run, only then he'd planned on taking Tony with him. But Tony was dead, and there could be no changing that fact. His intuition told him the time to leave had come. He rose, went to the bathroom to take a leak, then went to the kitchen, where he plucked the wireless phone from its charger.

"What's up?" Fernie stood in the doorway, his wide eyes on alert.

"You're taking a plane out of here this morning. To L.A. I'm making reservations for you at the Ramada in West

Hollywood. We need to get you away from here."

"How come? Are you in trouble?" Santos heard real fear in the boy's voice.

"You don't want to know, kid. You're going to have to trust what I say, OK? Just go get a shower and pack some stuff. You'll have to trust me on this," he repeated.

Fernie stared at him for a few moments, then turned to go.

Santos relaxed a little when he heard the shower start, glad the boy wasn't going to argue. There just wasn't time for debate. He flipped the phone open, powered it up, and dialed information.

Fernie worked silently in the bedroom, folding items of clothing and putting them neatly into two bags. These were the first nice things he'd ever owned, and he took meticulous care of them.

Santos stood at the kitchen counter and lettered an address onto a sturdy envelope, careful not to touch the paper with his fingers. Next he pulled on a pair of latex gloves, wiped the surface of a spool of tape, and dropped it into the envelope. He moistened the seal using tap water. The last thing he needed was a sample of his DNA in the hands of the police. He smiled to himself. The recordings of Davis's conversations with J.T. Mallory would sink the Nazi fuck without Santos ever laying a finger on him.

"OK, I'm ready." Fernie appeared in the doorway with a travel bag in each hand, his face serious.

"You're a cool kid, you know that?" Santos kissed him lightly on the forehead. "Let's get you to the airport. I'll explain what you need to do on the way. I just need to drop something in the mail on the way out there."

CHAPTER TWENTY

Santos pulled the Pathfinder into the right turn lane at the intersection of Airway and the freeway access road and waited for the traffic to clear. He'd just finished seeing Fernie off on a nonstop flight to L.A., making sure the kid had a list of directions in hand. Which shuttle to take, the number of the shuttle service, directions to the Ramada, precautions to take when going out alone in the city after dark, restaurants that were close to the hotel, on and on. Fernie had his own cell phone with 2,000 prepaid minutes, $4,000 in cash and traveler's checks in a wallet that stayed inside his pants, plus a decoy wallet in his back pocket. He also carried a copy of his birth certificate and social security card—everything he'd need to establish his identity if harassed by immigration at the airport.

"Remember, call me if you have any problems," Santos had admonished for the hundredth time. He even stood at the window with the anxious relatives of the other passengers, watching the beige and orange Southwest Airlines jet taxi down the runway and disappear into the sky. The tenuous thread of contact stretched until it finally snapped. Once Santos had trusted in thorough preparation and his own ability to handle the unforeseen, but since Tony's death he'd become a worrier. This morning he awoke on edge and the feeling hadn't dissipated, even after seeing Fernie safely on his way. Santos, who had always trusted his gut, knew that complacency killed as surely as lead. And today his senses remained on red alert.

Santos waited for a break in the stream of traffic and checked his rearview mirrors. Two cars behind him, a man on a sleek Suzuki glanced around the traffic, checking the progress of the line of vehicles ahead. Why didn't he just come around? There was more than enough room for a bike.

The traffic on the access road thinned, and Santos goosed the Pathfinder into the breach, easing toward the left to enter the freeway. Behind him the biker pulled around the waiting cars and entered the access road, trailing him at a distance. Santos removed his sunglasses and watched the rider closely in the mirror. In spite of the heat the man wore a dark full-face helmet and leather jacket.

Santos gunned the SUV up the entry ramp and into the freeway traffic, taking the middle of three lanes, with the passing lane open on his left and the slower merge lane open on his right. The Suzuki followed him up the ramp and tucked itself in behind a pickup truck a few hundred feet back. Santos eased down on the accelerator, still monitoring the bike, which, after a quarter mile, suddenly exploded into the left lane, gaining on Santos rapidly.

Santos punched the gas pedal to the floor and felt the Pathfinder surge forward. In the rearview mirror he could see the rider unzip his jacket and reach inside. The buzz-saw drone of the motorcycle's engine grew louder. Santos held the pedal against the floor but was coming up on a slower clump of traffic. In a matter of seconds there would be no way out. He glanced anxiously back into the mirror. The cycle had pulled up to within 20 feet of his rear bumper. The assassin's hand rose from the interior of his jacket, holding a machine pistol. The bike laid on a final burst of speed and began to pull even with Santos.

Santos counted one, two, three seconds, letting the bike gain on him, then whipped the Pathfinder into the left lane and slammed down hard on the brake. The SUV spun sideways, threatening to roll. The tires squealed and spewed smoke. The bike grazed the rear of the Pathfinder as the rider swerved to avoid hitting it. The bike skidded head-on into the concrete highway divider, the force of the collision catapulting its rider into an airborne cartwheel. The machine pistol fired wildly as the would-be assassin vaulted through the air. The man's upper body smashed through the windshield of an oncoming car, which lost control and spun end over end down the opposite side of the freeway. The riderless bike slid under an approaching tractor trailer rig and disappeared in a firestorm of sparks. All around, tires screamed as terrified motorists slammed on their brakes. Santos struggled to control the SUV, just managing to stabilize it before it flipped.

His hands were trembling. He headed for the nearest exit and parked in the shade at the edge of the parking lot next to Cielo Vista Mall. He gave the adrenaline coursing through him some time to burn off before lifting the tags from another SUV. From the mall he drove to a car parts store where he bought a replacement tail light. He pulled into an alleyway nearby and changed it out. Aside from the broken light the damage to the Pathfinder had been minor. The lane divider had taken the brunt of the impact. He thought about going back to the hotel, but decided against it. When the assassin failed to check in, the cartel would know their attempt had failed and would immediately field a team in an effort at containment. He drove instead into the twisting streets of a residential area, where he confirmed that no one was following him.

| ★ |

Jen ejected the 911 cassette from the tape player, lit up, and pondered her options. In the first place, she had a missing case file. Possibly not all that much out of the ordinary, paper records being what they were. Now, added to that, she had the ballistics report. The barrel signature on test rounds fired from Lyle Davis's gun were a confirmed match for several of the slugs taken from the bodies of the gay shooting victims. Whether Davis had actually pulled the trigger, they'd never know.

And now this. Mallory had shown up at the burned out ruins of Davis's house. And Mallory had filled out the report on the shooting. The 911 tape she'd just reviewed placed him at the scene of the shooting literally moments afterward. Jen couldn't believe it had taken her this long to think of pulling the tape. She looked at the phone records again. Davis had called Mallory's unlisted number on numerous occasions.

How had Mallory known Davis? Of one thing at least she was now sure: Mallory showing up at the ruins of Davis's house had not been simple curiosity about a case in which he'd been peripherally involved. But was it something more incriminating? She could make a case for coincidence and so, of course, could Mallory. Cops knew all kinds of people. Hell, she thought, *people* knew all kinds of people. Hadn't The Beach Boys known Charles Manson?

What should she do? Take it to Internal Affairs? The district attorney? If she did, just what exactly would she be accusing J.T. Mallory of? Certainly not murder. Conspiracy to commit? Prior knowledge? Being around too much? Talking to bad men? All she really had was a nagging suspicion, a hunch. But there could be no doubt about one thing: Everywhere she'd looked, Mallory had either been there already or shown up afterward. As far as Jen was concerned, this case had stretched coincidence thin enough to read through.

The beginnings of a conspiracy theory. That's all she had. She had nothing to support an accusation. And if she developed something, what if the I.A. division turned out to be sympathetic in the extreme to Mallory? The accusation would stick to her. Her case would be frivolous. She'd end up in sessions with a police psychiatrist. She'd be drummed out of the department, after which she'd be lucky to get a job as a school crossing guard. If she were advising another officer, she'd tell him to make damn sure the charge didn't come back to bite him in the ass. And if that officer was female? Forget about it.

She *could* take it up with her partner. Chuy kept a low profile and he'd been around for a long time. He at least knew the ropes. But he didn't have much longer to go before retiring. Would he close ranks? If he felt any outrage over the murders, it was news to her. As for the rest of the department, they were cops, weren't they? Cops didn't rat out cops for any reason. Period.

| ✶ |

The national news called it the largest drug seizure in history. Total worth as yet uncalculated, but estimated to be in the hundreds of millions. The story led on all the major networks and played incessantly on CNN, 10 full minutes with lead-ins that featured shots of busy border crossings, seemingly endless lines of trucks reputed to carry tons of drugs, and file pictures—none current—of Mexican drug kingpins. That same week *20/20* revived the Daniel Sexton assassination story, and *Frontline* did a complete hour on progress toward the legalization of marijuana and the overall failure of efforts to stem the flow of both soft and hard drugs.

A feeling of nervous exultation reigned in the various government agencies involved with drug interdiction. But the Sexton assassination had clearly established that when it came to drug enforcement, one could be too successful by half. Various agency heads were privately advised to increase security by no less than the Director of Operations of the CIA. A number of agents deemed vulnerable were quietly recalled to the States, and advisors working with the Colombian military were confined to their bases by direct order. If recent history was any gauge, everyone agreed, the cartel would hit back. Suddenly, mercilessly, and anonymously. The various agencies braced themselves and waited.

What didn't make the headlines was what a few middle echelon officers in military intelligence had recently discovered: Six surface-to-air missiles of advanced design were unaccounted for. True to form, that knowledge never made it off the reservation. The mid-level kept its collective fingers crossed, hoping for a simple inventory error, for a transfer to some other post before the shoe dropped, or for plausible deniability when and if someone somewhere brought down a plane. With sensitive budget negotiations stalled in committee, they all agreed that the Services didn't need some liberal cocksucker in Congress raising questions about missing high-tech armaments. Revelations, if any were ever forthcoming, would be timed for optimal damage control.

| ✶ |

The twin engine plane fueled at a decommissioned airport outside of Lordsburg, New Mexico, thumped lightly over the pitted runway, and rose into the moonless night, charting a course south-by-southwest. The scattered lights of Agua Prieta passed under as it slipped into Mexican air space. South of Agua Prieta, the craft veered south-by-southeast, flying beneath the crest of the Sierra de la Madera, below the sight line of Mexican radar, then swung due east, touching down at a private airstrip in Colonia Juárez, an affluent gated suburb west of Nuevo Casas Grandes. Here it took on fuel and a new passenger, Manuel Obregón, a special agent from the *Procuraduría General de la República*, the Mexican equivalent of the Attorney General's office.

The last time John Cunningham had seen Manny Obregón, his friend was strapped into a deck chair to prevent him from being pulled overboard by a swordfish he'd hooked off the coast of Todos Santos. A framed photo of the event hung over the desk in Cunningham's Washington office: Manny's thinning hair matted to his scalp by salt spray, the cords of his thick hands straining as he reeled in the line, coaxing the monster fish up from the sea. Cunningham regarded the trip as one of his better memories of Mexico. Tonight, however, they had bigger fish to catch.

As before, they'd be traveling together as "tourists," overflying the remote, mountainous geography of Sonora and Sinaloa, land of the opium poppy, cradle of Mexico's black tar heroin industry.

Under the soft glow of the plane's cabin lights, Obregón and Cunningham reviewed their respective briefings, glancing up from time to time to exchange questions and comments on the details of satellite photos and to pass pictures back and forth. In less than two hours they'd touch down in the coastal town of Guaymas for some much needed sleep. Cunningham stretched in his seat, and laid the briefing aside. It had been a long day. The next couple of days would be even worse.

In the cockpit the pilot established radio contact with the control tower at Guaymas, read off his position and speed, and prepared for a routine landing. At this time of night, no commercial flights would be competing for runway space.

On a hillside off the road between La Misa and the coastal highway, two Ford Explorers waited in darkness, their lights extinguished. The four men standing outside the vehicles strained to see, strained to hear. But they saw nothing in the sky but stars.

"*Dice que allí viene. No la ves?*" The Mexican army colonel grew increasingly tense with each passing minute. It seemed like they'd been out there forever. He peered into the darkened sky, his eyes aching, seeing nothing. If they missed this plane, there would be worse than hell to pay. Perhaps his source was mistaken. Another drop of sweat made a slow, cold journey down his side. The *patrón* had personally shot men for less, and in the colonel's presence.

"*No veo nada.*" The Colombian scanned the horizon with binoculars. "*Nadita.*"

"*Deben estar—*"

"*S-s-st. Silencio, con la chingada!*" The breeze carried the soft intermittent drone of a distant plane. The men strained to locate it before the sound faded again.

"*La veo, la veo!*" One of the men pointed excitedly toward a spot barely above the horizon. The running lights of an aircraft could be glimpsed.

The colonel shouldered the slender tube, flipped the switch that armed the device, and waited. The lights at the wing tips of the craft were clearly visible now, pulsing steadily. The Colombian zoomed in with his binoculars, lost the craft on the higher magnification, then regained it. The description fit. "*Es la avioneta,*" he pronounced, the tension apparent in his voice.

The steady drone of the plane's engines filled the night sky. The colonel lined up the tube with the approaching plane, put the craft in the sights, and pressed a small green button. The tube emitted a high pitched whine, not unlike a charging camera flash. A string of numbers fanned rapidly across the screen below the crosshairs of the sight and then abruptly stopped as the device acquired the target.

The plane flew almost directly over them.

"*Espera a que pase*," the Colombian whispered, as if the people aboard the plane might hear him.

"*Sí, sí, ya lo sé*," the colonel replied.

A green light flashed in the center of the crosshairs. The launcher was ready to fire. The colonel braced himself against the fender of one of the Explorers.

"*Dale! Dale en la puta madre!* the Colombian hissed.

The colonel pressed a large red button on the side of the tube. The dot in the crosshairs flashed red and the rocket fired. An orange flame, pencil thin, marked its flight path across the sky. The men held their breath as the missile hurled itself at its target. The initial explosion of the rocket hitting the cockpit, followed immediately by a brilliant white burst as the fuel tanks blew, created a double boom that reverberated across the hills and lit up the desolate countryside. Burning wreckage plummeted from the air, spinning in every direction.

"*Uujuley, qué avionazote!*" the Colombian exclaimed triumphantly. The four men high-fived. Shooting the plane down had been simplicity itself.

The colonel felt lightheaded, as though he might faint from relief. He slumped to the ground instead, hugging the warm launcher tube in his arms, his prayers answered.

]*[

Ron Colburn, the President's Chief of Staff, dreaded meetings with General James Smiley, the country's most recently appointed drug czar. The man's name itself was a joke. Colburn had never met anyone, even in the military, with less sense of humor. Not that this administration had anything to get all giddy about. The intelligence coming in could hardly have been more grim. The assassination of a high ranking DEA officer—in the driveway of his own home, no less—had been merely the icing on the cake of failure.

They'd have to make some hard decisions soon. The problem, Colburn realized, was that the shopworn rhetoric of the war on drugs had essentially narrowed their options to the use of force. Pulling away even slightly from the position of every previous administration would invite a battle with the drug hawks, James Smiley chief among them—a war Colburn knew no president could win.

Colburn waited in the hallway outside his office as Smiley marched—yes, the idiot was literally marching—in his direction. Christ, how had they ended up with this nut-job? Of course, he reminded himself, the appointment had been a compromise with the nut-jobs in the Senate. Smiley's face looked like "Onward, Christian Soldiers!" was playing in his head as he strode mechanistically down the hall. The sight of the robotic general gave Colburn the creeps. "James. Good to see you, as always."

The general took Colburn's hand in his moist grip.

It took all the control Colburn could muster not to recoil. "Come on in."

"I'm afraid I have some bad news." Smiley typically plunged into conversations without preamble. Colburn shut the door behind them, steeling himself. "I'm not telling you how to run your ship, but you may want to consider pulling Frank Morris in on this."

Colburn shuddered. Frank Morris, head motherfucker of NSC, the National Security Council. Great. Just great. This was Smiley's way of informing him that he was about to dump a huge load of shit into the administration's lap.

"So, what's up?" Colburn indicated a chair, and Smiley sat. At attention. Colburn took the other chair in the set, placing it at a psychologically comfortable angle to the general. He never sat behind his desk when speaking with ranking military. He'd been told the body language came across as too condescending, too confrontational. After all, these were territorial pack animals, their senses exquisitely honed to detect grades of status.

"The task force sent one of our men, John Cunningham, into Mexico at around 2100 hours yesterday, flying under their radar. Air Force pilot."

Colburn nodded. He knew Cunningham slightly. Clandestine insertion was now accepted policy between the U.S. and Mexico, a secret condition to the latest extension of Mexico's most-favored-nation status.

"In Mexico he met up with a man from the Mexican Attorney General's office, guy by the name of Obregón. We believe he's clean. Their plane's been shot down. No survivors. Mexican authorities confirm."

"Anything else, Jim?" Colburn scrutinized the general's impassive face. "I want the whole scoop of poop before I take this to the President. No last minute surprises. Any embarrassments will be shared." Would Smiley take umbrage at this threat? Colburn quickly decided he didn't care what the fuck this uniformed fool, rammed into the chair across from him, thought or felt. If, indeed, Smiley could be presumed capable of either.

"There may be one other wrinkle. I'm working to verify it. It's why I believe we should get Frank Morris in the loop." Smiley paused, then rubbed his forehead with his fingers, for the first time showing some sign of distress.

"I'm listening," Colburn said softly, assuming his best confessional manner while he waited for the general to drop the bomb.

"We think the missile that took them down may be one of

ours. I have a man who'd know for sure flying down there even as we speak."

Colburn took a deep breath. *I'm paid to think, not to shout*, he recited to himself. He braced himself to ask the next question. "So, how many of our missiles are out there, Jim?" He held his breath.

"We believe there are two unaccounted for."

Colburn started to ask to whom "we" referred, but decided to take a pass. For now.

"I guess you should know, from the start, that these are not conventional weapons we're talking about," Smiley continued. "They're smart rockets. The smartest."

"Yes, I think you're right, Jim," Colburn said, standing now, his voice crisp. "We should definitely pull in Morris on this. And Felder, from CIA, now that we think the hardware's gone over the border. We'll reconvene this afternoon, say 1500? Let's try for an initial damage assessment by then. I'll need to get this to the Chief."

The men shook hands again cordially. Within the next hour, Colburn knew, the general would see to it that the blame got spread around thinner than the peanut butter at a D.C. day care.

After Smiley had marched himself away, Colburn collapsed into his chair. "I am sick," he announced to the walls, "of living downwind of the fan this goddamn shit hits!" But what else could they do? Hell, in Plano, Texas, the upscale, relentlessly middle class town he and Sara had lived in before moving to Washington, three kids from one high school had died this year already from heroin overdose—with the school year barely into the first semester. How could they stand by and let that happen on a national scale? It would be political suicide. The administration had to do something, even if it was wrong.

Colburn felt he could safely assume that Smiley had lied about the number of rockets gone missing. When called to accounts by civilians, pricks like Smiley lied instinctively. The military bred arrogant shit-heads like roadkill bred maggots. So how many of the lethal rockets had they really lost? At least twice as many as Smiley had confessed to and probably more. All they needed now was the shooting down of a plane-load of citizens. Colburn wondered how he could make Smiley's karma come around and rip off his nether parts. He dialed the number of his best Pentagon insider on a secure line. He guessed he'd start by giving Smiley's karma a nudge. The general's confirmation would be the pile of shit they could rub some senatorial faces in before this mess had con-cluded. After a brief conversation, he hung up, straightened his tie, and went to look for the Chief Executive.

CHAPTER TWENTY-ONE

The group had been penetrated. The explosion at the church established that beyond any possible doubt. They should have followed the man in the Jeep that night, Mallory thought, taken him when they had the chance and burned his goddamn eyes out with a blowtorch. Made him talk, then buried his ass in the desert. But they'd let him go. *He* had let the guy go. That was his call, and he'd called it the way he'd seen it at the time. But he'd seen it wrong. And now, here they were.

Mallory had contacted the other members while they were at work—those who had jobs—and told them what happened at the church, told them to go to ground. Talk to no one. He figured their home phones would be tapped. He certainly assumed his was. Nothing so crude that he could find it, of course. The feds could tap your phone right through the line. Not even the phone company would know.

The enlisted men at Bliss took the news calmly, like the pros they were. Some of the others were rattled. Hell, Mallory was a little rattled himself. Whoever had killed Lyle and blown up the church, they weren't planning on another Ruby Ridge or Waco, taking out a whole group at once. On television at that. No, they'd wised up since then. Kill us off one or two at a time, days or weeks apart, blurring the issue, keeping their agents in the shadows. Make it look like random violence, drug related murders, revenge against individuals. Mallory found it ironic that the government would turn the group's own strategy against it. He'd have never guessed them to be that smart.

Now Mallory sat alone in the dark, replaying what had happened over and over in his head, examining it from every angle until he was so tired his bones ached. The lights of a passing car shone through the drapes, swept silently across the wall, across Betty's picture. Betty, his wife of 23 years, who had been dead now for two years, 11 months, and 12 days.

He'd packed his bags. They were waiting on the floor of the walk-in closet. He could disappear at any moment. He'd spoken by phone with one of the leaders of the Idaho church. They were apprised of the situation. In anticipation of the inevitable need to go underground, he'd worked out his escape plans far in advance. Since the day-care shooting in Los Angeles, and the attack on the towers in New York, the movement had prepared for intense scrutiny by the government.

The kikes, homos, porch monkeys, and liberal gun-control freaks were all up in arms now, banding together. But meetings and marches and angry speeches were all they seemed capable of. The feds remained the real danger. They would stage a nationwide confiscation of weapons next. Everything he and the other leaders had predicted, prepared for, and warned others about was coming. Mallory could feel it building. But he knew white Christians would take this country back from the degenerates, Jews, and mud people. Or the best part of it, at any rate. Hell, let 'em keep this god-forsaken desert. They could rot in it. It was all Mexican anyway, overrun with the greasy brown bastards. Beyond saving. He put his beer aside, half finished. Tonight was no time for alcohol and fuzzy thinking. He had work to do.

In addition to his police issue flashlight, he took his old .38 caliber service revolver. The whole thing had started at Lyle Davis's place, so that's where he'd begin. It might well be true that there was nothing left after a fire that intense, but he had to know for certain. Darkness had already fallen by the time he left, and he drove around for almost 45 minutes, back-tracking from time to time to be sure no one was following him. He was through taking chances. From now on, assuming the worst would be the rule.

He'd gone over his car as thoroughly as he could under the circumstances, searching for tracking devices, no matter how small. As far as he could tell, they hadn't attached anything to it. But he could never really know. After all he was no expert, and the technology advanced almost weekly. He'd warned the group repeatedly against complacency, and believed in men taking their own advice.

Out in the desert, away from the glow of city lights, darkness ruled absolutely. No moon lit the sky. Overhead, the Milky Way shone like a mystical path of souls. Mallory parked his Pontiac on the concrete strips that had been Lyle's half-assed excuse for a driveway, leaving the headlights on to illuminate the burned-out ruins of the house. Mallory hauled himself from the car, flashlight in hand.

Somewhere in the distant blackness, a pair of coyotes sang and a yard dog barked savagely in response. The small hairs on the back of Mallory's neck bristled. Creepy goddamn place, the desert at night. Disorienting, somehow. Empty. He'd never gotten used to it. He missed trees, snow, rivers, rain in summer. He missed Idaho.

Mallory walked down the side of the house where the bedroom had been, playing the beam of the flashlight over the rubble. Lyle's furniture, whatever might be left of it, would be the logical place to begin his search. If anything had been planted during a break-in, the furniture would be the most likely place for quick concealment. Putting a microphone in a wall took time and considerable effort to effectively hide.

His thin flashlight beam picked out part of a bed frame, the cheap metal warped by the fire. He stepped gingerly through the burned boards, careful not to step on nails exposed by the flames. Laying the light to one side, he knelt by the frame and inspected it, turning it over in his hands, examining it carefully, inch by inch, looking for whatever the police might have missed. On one of the L-shaped side pieces he found something that looked melted adhering to the metal. He took his reading glasses out, adjusted them to the bridge of his nose, and held the metal close to his face, playing the beam of the flashlight over it.

He picked at the small, blackened blob with a fingernail, patiently chipping away the charred outer crust, unaware of the silent movement off to his side. His flashlight caught the glint of tiny wires. The coating had been plastic of some kind. He kept chipping it away, one tiny fragment at a time, the inner workings of the object emerging slowly in the beam of the flashlight. The clump had once been an electronic device of some kind—yes, he could see it now—a miniaturized microphone. He pried it from the frame and dropped it into his shirt pocket.

He rose and tossed the ruined metal away. Lyle's place had been bugged. Even the fucking bed had ears. That's how they'd known. Wired the phone, too, no doubt. Conversations recorded, calls traced, names and places learned, plans revealed. No secrets. Not even pillow talk. The answer to the next question, how they'd latched on to Lyle, still eluded him. Maybe they'd selected Lyle's place because of its isolation. Out here, who would know if someone broke into the neighbor's house?

Clearly, the group had taken security for granted. He'd been far too confident. He would never have guessed they'd run into something this sophisticated out here in this dumb-ass Mexican shit-hole of a town. Even with the precautions they'd taken, they'd been too lax, underestimated the degree of surveillance. The feds, he told himself again. The feds had turned the whole country into a prison.

His peripheral vision registered a stealthy movement in the shadows beyond his small pool of light. He wheeled around with his flashlight and shone its beam into the darkness. The coyote resembled a medium-sized skinny dog with an elongated, clever face. Its retinas flashed the light back to him for a moment before it turned and skulked away into the brush. The Indians called the coyote *The Trickster*. Another trickster had been out there in the dark—for how long now was anybody's guess—watching them, sneaking around, careful to stay downwind, ears up, smart and quiet, gray and hard to see. That trickster would be coming for Mallory next. An explosion, a silenced bullet, a knife in the back, a piece of cord around the neck. Maybe in his bedroom, or in his car. Or in an elevator, or a parking garage. He felt a sensation like ice water trickle down his spine.

] ✳ [

Lessing figured she could interview Neal Pearson with his parents around and find out nothing, or she could catch him by surprise and take her chances with the defense attorney. Those were her choices. Play a hunch and possibly taint the evidence, or do it strictly by the book and give him a chance to collect his wits and clam up. She decided to try catching him off guard. He was out of high school and old enough to be tried as an adult if he happened to be involved. So that made him fair game. And with the young guys, she'd learned, you just assumed their guilt, tossed it right in their faces like you already knew everything, and frequently they'd fold up, just like that, kicked in the nuts by a guilty conscience. Once age dulled the conscience, one turned to other tools to pry out the truth. Jen knew those tools too, and knew that if push came to shove, she'd use them in a New York minute.

She'd read somewhere that intuition was knowing without knowing how you knew. That had validated her instincts, helped her to trust her gut. Two guys killed by claymores, a third seriously wounded. And all of it related to the gay killings somehow. This kid might just give her another piece of the puzzle. She'd made surprise work for her before. Now she'd see if she could make it work with this punk Neal Pearson.

The schedule from the registrar's office told them Pearson should be out of class in a couple of minutes. Jen leaned against the smudged plaster wall and focused her attention on the classroom door, as if willing him to appear. Three narrow vertical panes of glass. Chipped white paint. Behind that door a bored freshman class studying sociology in room 132. So normal. That was the really scary part, the apparent normalcy. Young killers, vicious sociopaths, going to school just like everybody else. Arriving on your doorstep, smiling, to take your daughter on a date.

Chuy stood on the other side of the hallway, his hands behind his back, perusing a bulletin board. He was not enthusiastic in the least about Jen's scheme, but he was giving her the benefit of the doubt for now. "At least you brought your partner in on it," he'd allowed. "At least *that* conforms to department policy."

The bell rang. Books slammed, chair legs scraped against floors, conversations began like a distant rumble. Instructors shouted last minute directions at fleeing pupils. A motley mixture of kids and adults of all colors, sizes, and ages poured into the hallway.

Jen spotted Pearson walking toward them. He was alone. That would make confronting him much easier. She strode toward the slouching figure and pulled her badge, catching him in mid step. "Neal Pearson?" She flashed the badge at his eye level, aggressively close.

The boy startled.

"Detective Lessing, El Paso Police. I need to speak with you. Now." A few students passing in the hall stared, but most seemed unfazed. Police presence in schools could hardly be considered an event anymore.

Desperation flashed in Pearson's eyes. He shot a glance back down the hallway, calculating his odds.

"Don't even think about it, young blood." Acevedo appeared at the kid's side, his grip biting down like a pipe wrench on Pearson's arm. The burly cop didn't have to spell out what could happen if Pearson ran. His tone of voice said it all.

"What the hell's goin' on? Whaddya want me for?" Pearson's backpack sagged in his hand.

"We'll be asking *you* the questions for now, Neal," Jen said flatly. By using his first name, she'd put him psychologically into the role of a child, a role he had still not completely outgrown. The kid's body language told Lessing he knew what they wanted him for, even if they didn't yet. She and Chuy moved him steadily toward an exit. "How long did you know Lyle Davis?" she asked.

"I didn't have anything to do with that!" Pearson blurted out angrily.

"Yeah?" she challenged. "With *what*, Neal? Blowing his guts all over his kitchen or helping him shoot those two guys?" They were almost at the stairs now, the exit in sight. She kept her hand on his back, hurrying him, almost pushing him along.

"I didn't hurt Lyle," Neal choked, close to tears. "I'll fucking kill whoever did that to him!"

"Like you killed those guys that night?" she demanded. "You did that sure enough, didn't you?" Lessing snatched him to a halt, stuck her face right into his. "*Talk* to me, badass boy! You hurt *them,* didn't you?" Lessing punctuated the question with a hard shove that bounced Pearson against the wall. Her instinct told her that hammering him relentlessly, keeping him off balance, would get results. She made Pearson for a bully, a coward, the kind who would crack without the support of others. And she had no intention of losing the initiative. "*Didn't* you?"

"I didn't shoot those goddamn faggots," the boy spat.

"Who said anything about faggots?" Lessing spat back. "You say anything about them being faggots, Detective Acevedo?"

"No ma'am. Not me. Mr. Pearson here identified them as faggots." Chuy's voice had acquired the nasty edge it always did when people fucked with him. Chuy was a real cop's cop when it came to shit like this. Might as well try to blow brimstone up the ass of The Lord High Executioner Himself as try to fuck with Chuy Acevedo. His grip on Pearson's arm tightened. The kid winced.

Jen took Pearson and turned him around, pinning his chest to the wall. "Spread your legs!" she demanded. She slipped the cuffs on his right wrist, her left hand between his shoulder blades, and began to Mirandize him. She felt his body shift, telegraphing his intentions. The kid wheeled around with his left elbow, intending to slam it into her face. She blocked with her left arm, felt his blow land harmlessly. She brought her knee up, hard, into his crotch. Pearson emitted something that sounded like an oink and doubled over.

"Thanks, jerk-off," she hissed in his ear. "You just assaulted an officer and resisted arrest. You try that again and I'll kick your goddamn brains down the street like a can."

Jen spun Pearson back against the wall. "You have the right to remain silent," she repeated, starting over. "You have the right to an attorney. Anything you say can and will be held against you in a court of law…" She snapped the cuff to his left wrist and yanked him up on tiptoes, levering his bony wrists with the cuffs, while she continued the recitation of his rights.

The cops pushed the much subdued Pearson ahead of them into the street, the rush of students parting to let them pass, and stuffed him into the back seat of the cruiser.

"Kick your brains down the street like a *can?*" Chuy shook his head and laughed. "I like that. I'm gonna use that."

As Chuy pulled the car away from the curb, Jen focused on the brown brick bell tower that served as the logo of the community college, forcing herself to breathe slowly and deeply to recenter. She'd been right. Neal Pearson was a fucked-up throwaway. Dog shit on the shoe of society.

Anger, not justice, kept her on the job. She had more than enough insight to know that about herself. People who believed in justice were blind. Nothing that happened later ever unmade what had gone before. For Lessing, evil, like an infection, was something a person recovered from, or didn't. And like disease, you had to kill evil anywhere you found it, every day, in yourself or in others, before it killed the world. She took another deep breath, held it for a count of three, and let it out. Right now she needed to get her anger back in the box where she kept it. Then she'd calmly wring the facts out of Pearson.

After that, armed with whatever information they got from Pearson, they'd take a trip over to the hospital to interview Ronald Schneider. Today was the day she'd bust this case open. Jen could feel it. Exhilaration bubbled up through the rage in her chest. *Score one for you, cousin Jack, wherever you are,* she thought. She didn't know whether to laugh or cry. She felt like doing some of both. Instead, she looked out the window of the car and waited to calm down.

When they got back to the station, she found a neatly lettered envelope in her mailbox. She shook it on the way back to her desk, where she sat down and opened it while they left Pearson to sweat it out alone for a while in the interrogation room. The contents consisted of a single tiny spool of tape. There was no other communication. Having no idea what kind of machine to play it back on, she tagged it as evidence and gave it to the secretary to forward to the police lab.

CHAPTER TWENTY-TWO

Santos made it through the INS checkpoint in New Mexico hours before sunrise and stopped for breakfast at a truck stop in Los Lunas, a couple of stops south of Albuquerque. By 10:00 that morning, exhausted, he'd checked into a bed and breakfast near downtown Santa Fe. When night fell the temperature dropped, and he built a small fire with piñon logs in the cast iron stove. Santos sat motionless, savoring the richness of his cup of coffee, and watched the play of light on the patterns of the Navajo rugs, the hissing and popping of the burning logs the only sound.

He picked a tiny cassette from the table and turned it over in his hands. Tomorrow morning, he'd send it priority mail to the DEA facility in Fort Bliss, site of the agency's high-tech eavesdropping facility that monitored the communications of Latin American drug cartels. The cassette was a video record of the rifle sale that led to the assassination of Daniel Sexton. It was sure to stoke the wrath of the U.S. government, all the while providing specific targets for their pent-up frustration. The DEA's reaction would make life interesting for his former employers while he disappeared.

That night he walked downtown, selected a restaurant off the plaza, and lingered over the food. He strolled the deserted streets late into the night. The next afternoon, he took highway 84 north toward Abiquiu, watching the color of the hills unfold along the way. At Chama, he turned west toward Shiprock, on the move, filling his eyes and days with new things until the past began to slough off like snakeskin. Santos felt the heavy weight of obligation lifting, his debt to Tony paid. A couple of times he stopped to call Fernie, just to keep in touch.

] ✳ [

Since Gregorio had dropped 24 kilos, breathing came easier and the vague pressure he sometimes felt in his chest had almost disappeared. He figured he still had another 20 kilos or so to go. His doctor had assured him, in complete seriousness, that he was eating himself into an early grave. After Don Carlos had issued the order to shoot down the American surveillance craft, though, Gregorio realized his line of work might very well see him prematurely dead without any collaboration from his diet. The time to bail out had arrived. Who knew what they'd shoot down next? They'd reverted to the old ways of business. Power had made them stupid.

The silver United Airlines bird skimmed over Balboa Park, almost caressing the treetops, and bumped down lightly only moments later on the tarmac, thin blue smoke rising from the tires. Gregorio heaved a silent sigh of relief as the plane taxied toward the terminal. The steep descent into the San Diego airport always unnerved him. Why the hell didn't they fly in from over the ocean? And how often did they have to change those damn tires? Probably not as often as they should. That danger filled the world came as no news to Gregorio Olivares, ex-fatso—*El Gordinflón* to his former associates. Henceforth he would be *El Tiburón*, after a fearsome Mexican gangster he'd seen in a movie.

Gregorio walked purposefully toward the INS station and presented his documents, impeccable forgeries all. He gave a tiny smile of self-satisfaction as the agent waved him through after the most cursory questioning. A plastic surgeon here in San Diego was internationally famous for his weekend face lifts, and *El Tiburón's* new face awaited, prepaid, soon to be added to his new documents and his new body habitus. The old familiar Gregorio, prime target for both American cops and the Mexican cartel, became each day less and less conspicuous.

In two more weeks—bruising faded, thinner yet—he'd deplane at LAX and melt into the enormous pot that called itself Los Angeles. Hiding in plain sight. Hell, he smiled, there must be more Mexicans in L.A. than there were in Guadalajara. Los Angeles: Mexico's second-largest city. Mexico had lost California in a single throw fighting, but was winning it back barrio by barrio fucking, *ganando tierra a la mejicana.* Soon they'd own Angelopolis again, Rodeo Drive and all. He laughed softly to himself at the idea of the gringos doing yard work and clipping poodles for rich Mexicans.

Gregorio recalled how Santos, the *maricón*, had told him what would happen if his people ever shot down a plane. Well, they had. *Marica* or not, Santos had been right. The incident had received nonstop newsplay in both countries once the identities of the occupants had become known. Relations between the two countries were more tense than at any time since the Camarena fiasco in the '80s. The Americans were in the mood for hardball. It was a good time to get out. He didn't have enough money for an oceanside home in La Jolla yet—far too high profile for his purposes anyway—but he certainly had enough to set himself up in business in L.A.

"Thank you. Have a nice day," the woman said as he presented his baggage stub and steered his luggage toward the taxi stand.

"Have a good one," he replied magnanimously, honing his American vernacular.

He stepped from the terminal into the bright California morning and found a taxi waiting for him. A good omen, he thought. His first doctor's appointment was set for that very afternoon. He slipped into the back seat, pleased by his new maneuverability, as the driver loaded his bags into the trunk. He relaxed, contented, as the taxi slipped into the stream of traffic.

Southern California, where life was good. Things would be better here. If he ever got into trouble, he'd cut a deal with drug enforcement, get shuffled off into the witness protection program, keep his money, move to Miami, and hook up with some party babe, a real blond with a tight snatch and big tits. He knew enough about the cartel to bring down all their operations in northern Mexico; the DEA would make him the fucking *mayor* of Miami in exchange for what he knew. Gregorio stretched, still a little stiff from his plane ride, and turned to admire the shining glass buildings that lined the freeway. Yes, California was definitely the place.

The cab veered into an exit and slowed. The cabbie caught Gregorio's gaze briefly in the rearview mirror and flashed a smile at him through the Plexiglas partition. The vehicle labored as it moved up a steep hill away from the airport. The travel agency had booked Gregorio's room in a hotel on the beachfront, but the car continued uphill and away from the coast. Perhaps the driver knew a shortcut.

Suddenly, without warning, the taxi swung into an alley between two rows of commercial buildings, then surged ahead in a burst of speed. The driver tripped a switch and the doors locked as the cab lurched to halt, throwing Gregorio headfirst into the Plexiglas barrier.

Dazed, Gregorio regained his balance, touching the rapidly expanding goose egg on his forehead. He heard the front door of the taxi slam as the driver made a hasty exit. The sound refocused his attention. What the hell was the fucking idiot doing? He attempted to open his door, heaving his still considerable weight against it, but to no avail. He looked out the window in search of the fleeing driver. Two armed men had materialized from the back of one of the buildings. Gregorio cowered in the seat, his hands raised in a futile gesture of defense as the silenced machine pistols rattled out two clips through the exploding windows of the cab. One of the men lit a gasoline bomb and tossed it into the car atop their target's still twitching form. A searing orange ball of fire engulfed the taxi with a deafening *whump*.

| ✷ |

Santos sat on the west end of the verandah of West Hollywood's French Market restaurant, sipped coffee, and read the latest on the drug wars in the morning edition of the *L.A. Times*. After the downing of the clandestine flight, the hispanophobic senator who chaired the committee on foreign relations—a senility case with a long history of Dixie-style political slapstick—had issued a pro forma demand for suspension of diplomatic ties with Mexico. As usual, few people other than his backwater constituents were listening with anything more than resigned annoyance.

On top of that, in a province of eastern Colombia, four more U.S. advisors had been killed in a helicopter crash during a skirmish with leftist rebels—despite American and Colombian protestations that such a thing could never happen. Santos smiled to himself. Evidently, someone on the other side hadn't heard about the "no casualties" rule. In Cali and Bogotá, right-wing paramilitary death squads had stepped up their rampage of murder and kidnappings. As always the American military command in Panama denied that any Colombian army regulars or their U.S. advisors were involved in any way with the atrocities. Strictly speaking, the predictability of all this disqualified it as "news." Administrations on both sides of the border came and went, but the song to which they danced never varied. Santos had read the same news before, again and again it seemed. One day it was El Salvador, next Nicaragua, then Panama, then Argentina. Now Colombia. And always Mexico.

Santos decided he'd leave Fernie some extra money in case things didn't work out between the kid and his new West Hollywood boyfriend. Tomorrow Santos would board a shuttle bus to LAX, followed by a plane to Florence, Italy, where he'd light a candle for Tony in Santa Maria del Fiore under the majestic dome. He laid the paper aside and finished his breakfast while he watched the men pass on Santa Monica Boulevard. The men walking past locked eyes with the men eating breakfast, and the men eating cruised back. Day by day Santos felt himself slipping into the comforting to-and-fro of normal gay city life. But he couldn't afford the luxury much longer.

"Get you anything else?" Lupe, the pert Latina waitress, in whose section he usually made sure he sat, had been off the day before. But today he'd been in luck.

"Yeah. Another refill on the coffee, please." He'd take a while longer, review his plan, looking for flaws. He pondered his movements for the day and sipped, reluctant to leave. Santos would miss his small routines here, breakfast on the veranda with his favorite waitress, prolonged workouts at the gym. When he finally stood to go, he passed Lupe a $20 tip, a going-away present of sorts.

| ☀ |

Mallory parked on a side street next to the university campus, adjusted his shades, and pulled the bill of his cap down against the dazzling sunlight before hiking uphill toward the brown brick mass of the medical center. Ron Schneider remained in the intensive care unit, but his condition had been upgraded from critical to serious after a week of battling sepsis. Mallory passed through the automatic sliding doors, crossed the marble foyer to the elevators, and punched the button for Schneider's floor.

Once there, Mallory pushed open the swinging double doors of the critical care unit. Here and there, clusters of people hovered around beds that were surrounded by curtains to maintain the illusion of privacy.

"Schneider?" he inquired of the secretary at the desk.

"Bed 9," she replied without looking up from her computer screen. "Down there on your right."

"Thanks," he said. As he approached Schneider's cubicle, he spotted a pair of men's shoes below the edge of the curtain. Next to them, he glimpsed part of a sensible woman's shoe. Ron had visitors.

In the cubicle next to Schneider lay an unresponsive old man connected to a ventilator. Mallory stepped in next to the bed, pulled the curtain partially shut, and leaned on the rail, as if in contemplation of the mortality displayed before him. He glanced at the armband on the withered wrist, in case he got caught eavesdropping and had to produce the old man's name.

"So Mr. Farris was standing *behind* you when you entered the building?" A male voice that J.T. could not recall ever hearing posed the question.

"Well, yeah." Schneider responded, still sounding more than a little fuzzy. He was obviously not in the best of shape.

"You know Mr. Farris was injured very severely." That

was the understatement of all time, J.T. thought.

"Right. They told me he didn't make it." Even from where J.T. stood, he could tell Ron was underwhelmed with grief.

"Well, see, we were just wondering"—the male voice again—"how he got hurt so badly and you escaped with much less serious injuries. Since you were standing in front of him. Right in the doorway, you said. Any idea why that happened?"

"Hell, man, I ducked!" Schneider's voice gloated. J.T. felt like strangling him.

"That was a great move. Saved your life." Mallory instantly recognized the voice as belonging to Jen Lessing, the recently hired detective. "How did you know to do that?" Lessing had taken on a female-standing-in-awe-of-the-alpha-male tone of voice.

"I heard the fuckin' trigger," Schneider swelled. "I figure I must have tripped a wire or something, pushing that bucket through the door." J.T. swore to himself. Naturally some hick tornado bait like Ron would be sucked in by the admiring female act. Christ, what a fucking idiot.

"Does the name Wolfskins mean anything to you, Mr. Schneider?" The male voice again. Mallory held his breath. Something about the man's tone of voice said he already knew the answer to that question.

"Well...uh...it's a kind of like...a, uh, social club. For guys." The question had clearly blindsided Schneider.

"Like what kind of *guys*, exactly?" Lessing again, all trace of the admiring female routine gone now. Her voice had acquired an unpleasant edge that made J.T. wince. The inter-rogators had Ron off balance and the tone of the questioning suggested they already knew most, if not all, of the answers to the questions they were shooting at Ron. "Like just *white* guys?"

"Yeah, I guess so." Ron had traveled the distance from

bragging to insecurity in a heartbeat. "There ain't no law against that, is there?"

"No, no law against that at all. Not at all." The male voice again, calm and reassuring.

"You know someone named James Mallory?" Lessing asked.

For a moment J.T. thought his heart had stopped. But of course they would know. They'd had Davis's phone tapped. But hearing the mention of his name...he just hadn't thought about how that would sound.

"I might. I mean, so what if I do?" Schneider asked, wary now, but too late.

"Just asking," Lessing responded evenly. The cops wished Schneider a speedy recovery, and excused themselves.

Mallory's heart sank. The mere tone of Schneider's answers had told them all they needed to know. In fact, the whole interview sounded to J.T. a pro forma verification of information they already had. But who else could have talked? He'd warned Lyle about that goddamn vanity plate, and now it had come back to bite them in the ass. His mind raced. They'd done their interrogation like pros: warm and confiding one minute, cold and accusatory the next. The freeze-thaw routine left Ron's macho facade looking like a county pave job after a hard winter.

Mallory got a good quick look at the interrogators as they passed the cubicle where he stood faking his visit. Lessing he'd already identified from her voice. Acevedo, her partner, who hadn't spoken. And a second man. J.T. had seen him before, but couldn't recall his name. He belonged to the district attorney's office. His presence meant interest in solving the Davis case had suddenly surged.

Obtaining a search warrant for Schneider's place would be their next step. J.T. shuddered to think what that search would turn up. God only knew what kind of trophies

Schneider might have kept laying around. Hell, by this time tomorrow Schneider would be shackled to his bed frame, his rights read and his warrant served, with a police guard in constant attendance, a prime suspect in several ongoing murder investigations.

I've got to stop this, Mallory thought, almost out loud. He shot a glance around the curtain to be certain the cops were gone.

CHAPTER TWENTY-THREE

This time Mallory parked on a side street and entered the hospital through a door around the corner from the emergency room. The scrubs and name badge he'd lifted from the employee locker room that afternoon would work unless someone questioned him closely. He doubted that would happen. By this time of night the security guards would be one floor up in the coffee shop, taking a break between the eviction of the last of the visitors and the first clock round of the night shift.

Next to the locker room where he'd stolen the badge, he located a cleaning cart. Uncapping the containers one after another, he began a rapid inventory of their contents, cautiously passing the mouth of each bottle back and forth under his nose. The third container, a white plastic spray bottle, held a solution with a powerful antiseptic odor. He tilted it up and read the label. VIREX. As far as he could tell, guaranteed to kill anything. He pushed the cart out of the storage room and down the hall toward the intensive care unit.

Mallory pressed the square metal control switch on the wall that opened the door to the unit, and pushed the cart through. At the far end of the spacious area, a nurse sat next to a patient cubicle, hunched over, charting. Two other women in vividly colored floral scrubs talked animatedly in the glassed-in medication station, the only area that remained well-lit at this hour. They glanced in his direction, but barely noticed him.

He stopped by the first of the cubicles in the row leading to Schneider's bed, plucked a large plastic garbage bag from the bottom of the cleaning cart, and began methodically filling it with trash from the smaller bedside receptacles. In the first cubicle, he found a large syringe in a drawer of supplies. In the drawer beneath it he found a collection of needles, color coded by size. He glanced around as he quietly bagged the trash. None of the nurses were even in sight. He picked out a needle, in a pink wrapper. The thing was as thick as a piece of wire. He palmed the syringe and needle and moved on to the next cubicle.

He worked his way steadily toward his target, emptying more trash into the collection bag as he went. The cubicle next to Ron stood empty now, the black, plastic-coated mattress stripped of linen. Apparently the old man attached to the ventilator had finally died.

He stepped into Schneider's darkened cubicle where, concealed behind the curtain, he removed the needle from its protective sheath and twisted it onto the hub of the syringe. Next he plunged the needle through the wall of the plastic spray bottle and pulled back 50 milliliters of the blue disinfectant solution.

Schneider lay on his left side, snoring. Suspended on a metal arm that extended from the wall was a small television set with the sound off. Onscreen, images of a popular sitcom flashed in rapid succession. An IV pump worked silently at the side of the bed, pushing saline into Schneider's veins through an intravenous catheter that had been threaded into the side of his neck. Mallory found a rubber port in the plastic IV tubing close to where the line disappeared into the sleeping man's flesh, inserted the needle carefully into the rubber diaphragm, and rapidly injected the cleaning solution. He then withdrew the needle and concealed the syringe behind rolls of toilet paper on the second shelf of the cart. He added the contents of Schneider's trash can to the large collection bag and moved on quickly to the next cubicle. A frail looking, very pale old woman slept curled in the bed. Mallory slipped around the railing, careful not to wake her, and stood motionless, hardly daring to breathe.

Somewhere in the direction of the nurses' area an alarm emitted a series of loud bongs, three at a time, over and over.

"Shit!" a female voice shouted. "Stacey, nine's in V-fib!"

"Get the crash cart! Maria, call a code!" A different female voice with an authoritative tone. From behind the curtain, Mallory heard the approaching stampede of feet, the clatter of equipment, and the sound of Schneider's curtain running frantically around the rod.

"OK, get the pads on him! Where's respiratory?" Mallory heard the sounds of a table being moved and hands yanking open drawers and rummaging in their contents.

"Charging to 200," the authoritative voice said. Overhead a male voice announced "Code Blue, ICU...Code Blue, ICU...Code Blue, ICU" over the public address system. From the other side of the curtain, "Let that go! Everybody clear!" And then a pause followed by the thump of Schneider's contracting form as electricity surged through him.

"He's still in it! Three hundred!" The defibrillator whined as it built the necessary charge. "Everybody clear!" Another spastic thump of contracting limbs. Mallory caught a faint whiff of burning hair.

"Still V-fib!" someone called out. "Charge to 360!" Mallory heard the whine of the defibrillator, another thump, and a brief silence. The door to the unit opened noisily, followed by an inward rush of additional personnel. The cavalry had arrived. The elderly woman in the bed beside him continued her deep, regular breathing, her face sagging under the weight of sedated sleep.

"OK, start compressions." The take-charge female voice again, calmer now, a hint of resignation creeping in. "Somebody get an airway out of the cart. Push an amp of epi."

"Amp of epi, going in."

"What's going on?" a breathless young male voice asked. An intern, Mallory supposed.

A female voice rattled off the answer. "He's a sepsis case, injured during that church explosion that's been on the news, extubated two days ago, well...three days ago now, doing fine, stable vitals, no ectopy, ready to be transferred tomorrow, then just went into V-fib. Just like that, no symptoms at all. We've shocked him three times and haven't been able to convert him."

"Probably threw a clot. Pulmonary embolism," the doctor replied. Things didn't sound like they were going any too well over on Ron's side of the curtain, Mallory thought. He wouldn't be shooting his mouth off to any more cops, at least not in this life. J.T. slipped by the curtain into the last bed in the row, and stepped out into the open, trash bag in hand, nearly colliding with a hospital security guard.

"Mind waiting outside?" the uniform asked, looking a bit surprised.

"Not at all. No problem," Mallory responded. Trash bag in hand, he steered the cleaning cart through the double doors as a couple of men in scrubs rushed in. He shoved the cart into a utility closet, removed the syringe and needle and dropped them into a red plastic container for contaminated instruments. He smiled as he headed down the hallway toward the door and freedom. One less snitch with diarrhea of the mouth. He'd shut Ron up for good and never even left a mark on him.

Outside, the cool evening air and the bright rush of excitement put a lively spring in Mallory's step as he crossed the darkened parking lot on the way back to his car.

| * |

Lessing opened the top drawer of the battered clothes chest, and there it lay, with its Pachmayr grip exposed, jutting out from under a pile of mismatched socks like a big black thumb. "Chuy," she called. "Come in here a minute?"

"Whatcha got?" Acevedo's stocky figure entered from the adjacent room.

Jen nodded toward the contents of the drawer. "Take a look at this," she said.

Chuy peered over her shoulder. "*Híjole, Santa Madre Purísima, gracias a tí,*" he muttered, crossing himself. "This sure beats the hell out of writing parking tickets. Got something to lift it out with?"

"Yeah. Hold this bag open, will ya?" Lessing lifted the socks off to one side and slid the end of her ballpoint inside the trigger guard. She gingerly raised the blue steel revolver from the drawer and eased it into the plastic evidence bag.

"Think it'll match the other rounds?" Chuy asked as he scribbled out a label and stapled it to the mouth of the bag.

"I'll bet you my pension it does," Jen said.

The search of Schneider's apartment continued, with Lessing in charge of the contents of the bedroom. Drawer by drawer she worked her way through the chest but uncovered nothing else of interest. She turned to the bed but again came up empty-handed. She'd decided to toss the closet next when her partner stuck his head in the doorway.

"Hungry yet?" Chuy asked.

Lessing glanced at her watch. One-thirty already. They'd gotten the search warrant a little late. The judge had been tied up in court all morning and had finally called a recess so he could sign the document. "Not yet, Chuy," she lied. "Let me just finish this room, and then we'll take a break."

Acevedo disappeared, looking a little disappointed.

Lessing turned her full attention to the closet. Some work clothes in one section, casual pants and shirts next, a cheap out-of-fashion suit, probably left over from high school. And a crisp military uniform of some type, not new, but starched and very neatly pressed—obviously something Schneider had taken seriously.

She removed it and laid it out on the bed. A pair of cowboy boots lay tossed on the floor, the brown leather scuffed and worn down at the heels. Next she inspected a pair of treadless Nikes. In the corner stood a pair of black boots, shined to a high gloss. They obviously went with the uniform. She picked up the boots. Heavy. She examined them one at a time, closely. Steel toes. On the right one, deep in the groove between the leather upper and the sole, something dark had dried. "Chuy?" she called again. "Need another evidence bag. A big one, please."

CHAPTER TWENTY-FOUR

J axon's OK?" Lessing inquired.

"Sure," Chuy shrugged. "If you think two cops can afford it."

"My treat. I think we deserve a little celebration."

Frankly, she'd never expected to get this case off the ground. In fact, if people hadn't kept killing people, the initial investigation would never have reached critical mass.

While they waited for a table, she motioned Chuy over to a quiet corner of the lobby. "I want you to listen to me," she began. "I want you to tell me if we really have a case."

"That'll be up to the D.A.'s office, but yeah, I'll hear you out."

"OK," Jen said. "First, we have the phone traffic, beginning with Mallory calling in the shooting to dispatch. He's first at the scene. That could have been coincidence."

Chuy nodded in agreement.

"Next we have the phone records from Davis's place," she continued. The D.A. had subpoenaed the phone records of all the principals in the case. "The phone records show that Davis and Mallory called each other daily, sometimes more, during the time of the murders."

"That shows that Davis and Mallory had some business together," Chuy said. "But it's not incriminating if Mallory can show that the relationship was innocent."

"Which he won't because he can't."

"Agreed," her partner conceded.

"And then there's the tape. Recordings of Davis and Mallory conspiring to commit murder. But there's a problem. Defense will file a motion to exclude on the grounds of provenance."

"Which will be denied," Chuy said. "You didn't find it, solicit it, trade favors for it, or put out for it—and if you did, I don't want to know about it," he added with a smirk. "And your chain of custody is intact. It showed up in the mail, you opened it, tagged it, and turned it over to the lab."

"So there's no question we have Mallory conspiring to commit."

"No question," he agreed. "Plus, you have the photo of Mallory at Davis's place after it burned down. Which means next to nothing from an evidentiary standpoint, but puts him there in the mind of the jury."

"And then we have ballistics. The pistol in Davis's car matches slugs taken from De La O and his boyfriend. We don't even need the rounds taken from the wall."

"But defense will argue that the shooters were merely aiming at the wall that night, and De La O and his boyfriend just happened to walk into the line of fire," Chuy replied.

"I wouldn't put it past them," she said, smiling and shaking her head. "We also have Pearson's confession, which implicates Mallory, Davis, Schneider, and that guy Farris in the shooting. Anything else?"

"Davis and Farris are dead," Chuy observed. "We don't have that angle figured out. And forensics is still cooking the stuff we took from Schneider's place. That'll give something up, you can bet on it."

Jen nodded. If the substance on Schneider's boot turned out to be blood, DNA sequencing could prove if it had come from the cross-dresser beaten to death in the park. "That," she said, "is the good news. Now what's the bad news?"

888

"The original case file's lost," Chuy replied flatly. All efforts to find it had failed.

"And we don't know who killed Davis. Or bombed the church," Jen added.

"But that has nothing directly to do with Mallory. He's still guilty as sin," Chuy reminded.

"True. But it's still loose ends. And at some point we're going to have to deal with that."

"You think De La O did it."

"Who else?" Jen asked. "Problem is, De La O and the Fernandez kid are gone. We don't know where the fuck they are."

"That's a problem," Chuy acknowledged.

"I *know* De La O did it. But we have no evidence. Zilch. So even if I had him sitting here in front of me, I couldn't hold him." Jen shrugged. At least they'd bagged Mallory.

Now that police implication in the crime had been proven to the D.A.'s satisfaction, he was pushing for rapid analysis of the evidence gathered from Schneider's place. Internal affairs had pushed hard for a preemptive strike. Remove Mallory completely and swiftly while the case was still contained. Otherwise, the department could face the loss of precious credibility and community good will. Or, worse yet, intervention by the Justice Department. There would be no LAPD-style cluster fucks in this city's law enforcement. The D.A.'s office had made that crystal clear.

If the evidence from Schneider's apartment linked him to the slayings, the D.A.'s office and the police command had agreed that both Schneider and Mallory would be arrested immediately. If not, Mallory's arrest would be delayed another 24 hours while the evidence hardened. The D.A. intended to move that Mallory be denied bail but wanted incontrovertible evidence of his involvement in the event the court was predisposed toward leniency.

"Well," Chuy observed. "You'll roll that prick Schneider over. I'd put money on it. You got that Pearson punk singing like a canary in heat."

Jen smiled at the compliment. Here, at this moment, Lessing felt a rising tide of exultation sweep over her. Right now, maybe just for today, she loved this job. Tomorrow would probably be a different story.

Chuy's cell phone trilled, and he extricated it from the depths of his coat pocket. He spoke for a moment, the expression on his face darkening. He flipped it shut and dropped it in back in his pocket.

"Need to tell you something," he said, nodding toward the door that lead to the porch.

"What's up?" Lessing asked, though something in her partner's eyes told her she really didn't want to know.

"Let's talk outside," he said. They walked back out into the sunlight and stood by the railing of the porch. "That was the office. Schneider's dead. Died suddenly last night. They couldn't get him back."

"But that's crazy," she said, struggling to assimilate the news. "He was doing so well."

How badly did this hurt them? she wondered. They'd been about to break the case wide open. They already had Pearson, and they'd fully expected Schneider to both corroborate and enlarge on the boy's testimony.

"Yeah, I know," Chuy said, shaking his head in disbelief. "They think he threw a clot or something. They say it happens sometimes."

"Are they at least getting a post?"

"Didn't say."

Acevedo looked downcast, Jen thought. He'd become interested in the case, particularly after J.T. Mallory's name had come up. Something about Mallory had clicked with

Chuy, but he hadn't elaborated and Jen hadn't asked. "Schneider's a principal suspect in a homicide investigation, and suddenly he dies? They'd damn well better do a post mortem!" She wanted a smoke and wanted it bad. "Screw it. Let's eat. At least one thing's going to go right today."

"What about Mallory? Think we should request a stake-out on his house?"

"Good idea. But lets wait till the ballistics report comes back. That will tell us if Schneider's really a shooter, or if Pearson's just bullshitting. Cover your ass, right?"

"Definitely," Acevedo replied. "Personally, I don't think the Pearson kid could bullshit a Sunday school teacher, but it can't hurt to be sure. Besides, where is Mallory going to go?"

| ✳ |

Neal looked across the metal table at his public defender and waited. Neither the situation nor his lawyer looked very promising.

Gerald Fortner's bony fingers nervously shuffled a stack of documents, arranging and rearranging them. The young lawyer cleared his throat, clearly unsure how to proceed. Finally, he looked up at Neal, made momentary eye contact, and spoke. "Well, basically, Neal, the district attorney's office is trying this as a capital murder case." Fortner cleared his throat for the sixth or seventh time and fidgeted with the stack of papers, avoiding his anxious client's gaze.

"What does that mean?" Pearson asked, wondering if they could have found a bigger pussy than this guy to defend him. At least Fortner wore a wedding ring, which meant he wasn't a total fag.

"It means that they have this confession, for one thing. Which it appears you gave of your own free will." Fortner shook his head in disbelief. "And it means they have corroborative evidence, more of which appears to be emerging as we speak."

"Jesus," Pearson hissed. "I mean what does *that* mean? For *me?*"

Fortner visibly winced.

Christ Almighty, Pearson thought, *this skinny jerk was his defense?*

"It means they can establish planning and prior knowledge. It means they have a very damaging confession here." From his tone of voice, Fortner almost made it sound like *he* had been the one to confess to a double homicide. "I imagine the D.A.'s office is out looking for further evidence that supports your confession. That will make it impossible for you to back out."

"That bitch of a cop *threatened* me," Neal shouted. "Her and her goddamn greaser partner."

"A jury might not see it that way," Fortner replied, his face coloring. "If they have the testimony of other conspirators and physical evidence, your confession will just be added proof that you intended to kill those men."

"You don't even believe in me yourself, you skinny fruit!" Pearson shot back.

"Maybe it would be more productive to have this conversation another time," Fortner said, standing. "Perhaps by then you'll calm down and be able to speak to me without insulting me."

"Fuck you!" Pearson spat. He'd made Fortner mad now. At least the goddamn pussy wasn't wringing his skinny fingers and stammering anymore.

"Fine!" Fortner said, slamming Pearson's file down on the table. "Let me explain very clearly what I'm seeing here. I'm seeing a *punk* who gave a very cool, very detached videotaped confession to the murders of two people he'd never even *met!* People who had never threatened him in any way. I'm seeing a hard sell to a panel of people who are sick of hearing about gratuitous brutality and murder on a daily basis. Sick of hearing about people like *you,* Mr. Pearson. Your best hope— your *only* hope in my opinion—is that the prosecutor's office will let you plea-bargain in exchange for your testimony. They might also consider your age, but I wouldn't count on it. In case you've forgotten, Mr. Pearson, you're in Texas! Juries here are not exactly squeamish about handing down death sentences."

"So it's bad, huh?" Neal asked.

Fortner stared at him without saying anything for several moments, then closed his eyes and shook his head. "I'll see if they'll make a deal based on your cooperation. Right now I can't talk about this any more," he muttered, turning to leave. "You just better hope to God there's someone you can blame this on," he added without looking back.

Pearson swallowed hard. Lethal injection. It was like putting down an old dog. No big deal—except maybe to the dog. Ron, who was hardly his friend, was in the hospital. Lyle, who had been his friend, was dead. J.T., who was a cop, hadn't even shown his fat face in here the whole time. Neal's mother had been his only visitor. Right now he just wished he was somewhere else.

CHAPTER TWENTY-FIVE

L essing." She'd caught the phone on the first ring.

"Good morning, Detective. John Barker, Forensics. How ya doin' this morning?" Barker sounded pleased. Either the man suffered from pathological early morning cheerfulness, or he had information he thought she'd want to hear.

"Fine. How are you, John?" Although she'd never met Barker, for some reason she found herself on a first name basis with him.

"Great, thanks. I've got that ballistics report you wanted. Looks like a perfect match. The test shots from Schneider's pistol? Excellent match with two of the slugs they dug out of that kid at autopsy."

"So you'd testify to that in court?" she asked.

"No problem. Set a date, I'll be there."

"Could you fax that report over to me? I'll need to go over it with someone this morning."

"Sure. It's on the way. You should be getting it in a couple of minutes."

"Great." She started to hang up. "John? You still there?"

"Yeah?"

"Thanks, OK? Strong work." She hung up, took a deep breath, and dialed the office of the D.A. The secretary answered. "Is Mr. Samaniego in? This is Detective Lessing. He's expecting my call."

"I think he just went back to his office. Let me try to connect you." The extension rang repeatedly while Lessing waited.

"Jackson here." Lessing recognized the voice of one of Samaniego's staff of prosecutors.

"Good morning. This is Detective Lessing in Crimes Against Persons. I need to speak with Mr. Samaniego, please. He's expecting my call."

"Sure. Hang on a sec, OK? I'm putting you on hold." Before she could protest, the line went silent. She resisted the urge to swear. The assistant D.A. had sounded harried.

"What's up Jen?" Samaniego asked, picking up the line.

Lessing took a deep breath. "The ballistics report on Schneider's pistol just came back. The test rounds match two slugs recovered from the kid shot in front of the gay bar. Neal Pearson claims Schneider was in the car that night, and that he borrowed Schneider's pistol. So the ballistics verify that version of events. I think his confession's good. I can also link the suspects through phone records. We also have Mallory's conversations with the other principals on tape. I think we have enough to issue a warrant for Mallory's arrest."

Samaniego said nothing for a few moments. Jen could almost hear his wheels turning. Finally the D.A. spoke. "You ever figure out who sent us the tape of Mallory's calls?" he asked warily.

"Someone mailed it to my office. Anonymously. No prints, not on the tape, and not on the envelope. *But*," she emphasized, "*we* did not record this, nor did we solicit anyone else to do it for us. We had nothing to do with the production of the tape. So it's admissible evidence. We don't have to show probable cause." You just lectured the District Attorney on admissible evidence, she told herself. Here's hoping he's not some macho prick. Samaniego said nothing for a moment about this incredible windfall. Jen caught herself holding her breath.

"I'll bring Internal Affairs up to speed." Samaniego paused again, weighing his words. "And I have another wrinkle for you, Detective. I made Schneider a coroner's case, for reasons that are obvious. The toxicology is still pending, but the M.E. tells me that there was no pulmonary embolism. And no heart attack, no stroke. In other words, no reason he could find for the guy to croak out like he did. So we're not ruling out the possibility of foul play. Your instinct about this case so far has been good."

"Thank you," she said. It looked like the D.A. had chosen to overlook her law lecture.

"So we're going on the assumption of foul play," Samaniego continued, "at least until we can exclude poisoning. Unless someone dosed him with potassium chloride, which has happened in hospitals. In which case, I'm told, we'll never find it."

"We checked that angle," Lessing interjected. "Their pharmacy issues potassium chloride on a strict per dose basis, and only with a doctor's order. We went through the records with the hospital's risk manager. All the potassium chloride issued by the pharmacy since Schneider's admission was accounted for. Unless someone falsified the records, which we doubt. Anyway, no one ever ordered any of it for Schneider. His potassium levels were never a problem."

"You can probably buy it off the shelf in any drugstore in Juárez," the D.A. replied. "You can get about anything except narcotics over the counter there. I know because that's where I get my wife's prescriptions. For narcotics, you don't even need to go to the drugstore," he added. "That stuff you just buy on the nearest street corner."

Lessing gave a short laugh, even though it didn't sound like the D.A. had intended the remark to be funny.

"So anyway, detective, we'll meet in your office with a man from I.A. at…let's say 11:30. That work for you?"

"Absolutely."

"OK, done. See you then." The D.A. hung up. Lessing dropped the receiver softly into the cradle and sat quietly, thinking. In the strangeness category, she doubted anyone could top these past few months. Her partner's arrival put an end to her musings. She motioned Chuy over to the desk and filled him in on the plan for the day.

| ✳ |

J.T. Mallory inspected the last suitcase and glanced at his watch. Already going on 1 in the afternoon. He took a quick walk through the house and plucked the last of his wife's pictures off the piano. Not only had he never learned to play, he'd never even raised the cover that protected the instrument's keys. The piano had been Betty's fascination, not his.

He looked around one last time. For a few moments he forgot his urgency and stood staring at her picture in his hand. The uncomfortable feeling of having forgotten something essential struck him every time he packed for a trip, but especially now since he was making his last trip away from the home they'd shared. From the soggy northwest to the bone dry desert. For a few years the change of climate had helped her breathing, but eventually her emphysema had run her to ground, gasping helplessly.

He walked back to the bedroom, tossed her picture onto the pile of clothes in the suitcase, closed the lid, and snapped the tabs. From the bed next to the suitcase, he scooped up his old .38 Special and dropped it into the pocket of his windbreaker. He needed to get out of here. *Now*. Put some serious distance between himself and this town. At least he'd shut Schneider's mouth. Ron could have betrayed any number of people. He knew too much about the members. But how could he shut Pearson up? With the kid in custody, there didn't appear to be any way. He guessed he had no choice but to let the kid go and take the consequences of his desertion.

Mallory picked up his suitcases and headed for the garage, holding the larger case in his left hand, the smaller one under his arm, his right hand free and his full attention on his escape. The feds would have to have his conversations with Lyle on tape. Why they'd waited this long to make their move on him, he couldn't guess. He glanced at the kitchen clock as he opened the door to the garage. Sixteen minutes after one. A few more minutes and he'd be on the interstate, headed north. Let them try stopping him then.

He tossed his luggage into the back, slid behind the wheel, and started the car. As he backed out into the driveway, he saw them. An unmarked car with three people in it and a black-and-white cruiser with a single officer. The black-and-white pulled across the driveway, cutting off his escape. They'd waited until the last minute to play their hand.

Mallory stopped the car, reached into his jacket pocket, and pulled out the .38. Well, if they wanted it now, by God they'd get it. Instead of fear, he felt relief. He opened the car door and stepped out, pulling back the hammer of the pistol and easing the gun behind him, out of sight.

| ✳ |

"Shit," Lessing muttered as the car pulled to a stop. "He's making a run for it."

"Mike'll block him," Acevedo said. On cue the patrol car

in front of them pulled across Mallory's driveway and braked.

"I don't like this, Chuy."

Even as Lessing spoke, the patrol car's door opened and officer Mike Warren got out.

"Wait for us, goddamn it! Wait!" Lessing pushed the back door of the car open as she released the hammer strap of her holster.

Warren walked around the front of the cruiser and up the driveway toward Mallory, smiling as he approached. "J.T., how's it hangin'?" he asked.

Without warning, Mallory raised his arm and pumped three rounds into Warren's chest. The patrolman staggered backward and fell, sprawled on the concrete.

Lessing lunged out of the cramped quarters of the back seat, struggling to free her sidearm, using the car for a shield. "Drop it!" she screamed at Mallory. She saw Warren, one arm flailing weakly in an expanding pool of red.

On the other side of the car, Chuy's door burst open.

Mallory swung toward them and opened fire. A round cut a groove into the top of the car, inches from Lessing's face. She fired back, squeezing off shot after shot.

Mallory fired once more.

On the other side of the car, Chuy spun and went down, still struggling with his holster, blood spreading across his shirt.

"Goddamn it!" Lessing screamed. Mallory should have one more shot, she realized as she emptied her clip. She had never been so frightened in her life, or so murderously mad. She saw Mallory stumble backward and clutch his chest as he fell. Her hands shaking, she slammed in a new clip, chambered a round, and paused to assess their damages.

The assistant D.A. cringed in the front seat. He'd come unarmed.

"Out!" Lessing snapped. "Get out here!"

Holding her firearm with one hand, she quickly peeled off her jacket, and, pulling the trembling assistant D.A. behind her, circled the vehicle to where Chuy lay in the street. He attempted to sit. "Lay down," she ordered, pressing the jacket against his chest.

"Ouch, goddamn it! That hurts!" He attempted to sit again, but Lessing pushed him back.

"Lay still! You're bleeding." She turned to the assistant D.A. "Here, hold this," she told him, placing his hands on the wadded jacket. "Press it down tight." She stood, slowly, gun extended. She couldn't see Mallory. She found her cell phone and called for backup, even though half the neighborhood had probably called the cops by now. She dropped into a low crouch and moved forward behind the patrol car. From her new vantage point she could see Warren from up close. His chest wasn't moving. A rapidly expanding pool of blood spread around him and ran down the driveway into the gutter.

Behind Warren, Mallory lay motionless in the yard. Keeping Mallory in view, she made her way to Warren's side and searched for the pulse that was no longer there. Mallory lay on his back, arms extended. His nearly empty service revolver lay beside him in the withered grass. She rose from Warren's side, keeping her gun on Mallory, and walked toward him. She kicked the revolver away and stood over him, her pistol aimed at his heart. His ragged breaths came out like rasping, shallow panting. Like a sick dog, she thought. He coughed, spraying blood into the air. His eyes slowly focused on hers. "I'm hit," he whispered. "Help me. I'm bleeding bad."

"Yeah," she said flatly. "You're bleeding. That's how you're going to die, asshole. You're going to lay there and bleed to death. Just like Warren." Jen stood, looking down at him, her mind churning. Then she bent closer and forced a smile. "That fag killed your boys, you know that?" J.T. stared up at her, his pale face contorting with anger. "Yeah, Mallory. That *fag* killed Davis, killed Farris, and sent us a recording of your phone calls. You pussy loser! Beaten by a *queer!* Cook on *that* while you finish bleeding to death."

Jen turned and walked away. Somewhere in the distance, sirens screamed. Mallory coughed again and gurgled blood. Jen didn't bother to look back.

| ✳ [

She sat in the semidarkness, her fourth scotch on the rocks sweating coldly in her hand. Slivers of daylight probed the spaces in the blinds, but faded and died before reaching the chair where she sat curled. Alone. So glad to be alone. Fred had gone to the office at her insistence. He needed to keep busy. And she needed to be alone. She sipped her drink and tried to succumb to the urge to sleep, but the events of the day before intruded. Her phone trilled. She glanced at the caller I.D., but the device hadn't read the number. She waited for the caller to hang up, but the phone trilled again and again. Finally she gave up. "Hello," she said, unable to keep the exasperation from her voice.

"Good afternoon, Detective Lessing. I'm glad I caught you at home. Hope this isn't a bad time. I just wanted to know how the case is going."

"Which case is that?" she asked. The speaker's voice sounded mechanical, but the cadence seemed somehow familiar. Lessing realized the voice was being filtered through an electronic device to prevent recognition. But she knew she'd spoken to this person before. She was sure of it.

"The case of J.T. Mallory, of course. I assume you received my tape."

Lessing sat upright so suddenly her drink splashed across the upholstery. "Who is this?" she demanded.

"Let's say I'm a party with a material interest in the case, and leave it at that. So, have you gone after Mallory or haven't you?"

"Listen up, whoever the fuck you are. I don't have time for your games. If you're curious, read the papers like everybody else." Lessing hit the end button and held it until the phone powered down. She'd never felt more exhausted. She dropped the phone on the carpet and stood unsteadily. It was time, she decided, to pour another drink. She headed toward the kitchen, weaving slightly as she walked.

| ✳ |

Santos sat on the balcony in a corner, his back to the ancient stone, the city below him. He unfolded the laptop and logged on to elpasotimes.org. The story of the internecine police shoot-out had made page one, above the fold. The breathless reportage recited the known facts about "the bizarre chain of violent deaths." So Mallory had killed Schneider himself, murdered him while he lay recovering in the hospital. Santos shook his head in disbelief. Insane, all of them. And all accounted for now but one. Only the boy, Neal Pearson, remained, and he sat in jail, any possibility of bail denied, awaiting trial.

Santos set the laptop aside and raised a glass to vengeance. It wasn't exactly justice, but it would have to do. Then he rose, walked to the railing, and stretched, savoring the warm Tuscan air.

CHAPTER TWENTY-SIX

My oldest son, Rogelio—he has a real estate agency out in San Diego. He's trying to get us to move out there as soon as the doctors release me. He claims he can get us a great deal on a house." Chuy laid his fork aside, clearly finished. "The weather out there is wonderful. Cool at night, warm during the day. No winters. No summers either. Not like here. This summer's here are hotter than the hinges of hell. That was great, Jen," he added.

"And some great golf courses," Fred Lessing interjected. "Especially up in Palm Springs."

"I never learned to play," Chuy replied.

"So now you'll have time," Fred said. "It gets you out of the house, keeps you walking, gets you out in the air. I swear, golf's the only thing that kept my dad alive after he retired."

"Other than his wife," Jen added.

"Other than his wife," her husband agreed.

"I intend to get him out of the house and working in the yard," Laura Acevedo said. "Our kids, they have beautiful yards. Everything grows out there. It never freezes."

"So how did you do with the retirement board?" Jen asked, hoping to steer the conversation away from homes and gardens.

"Full benefits," Chuy answered. "They took into account that I'd been shot on the job and ignored that it was my own damn fault. So I guess in a way Mallory did me a favor. Early retirement, full benefits before I got myself killed by some *cholo*."

The two couples fell silent for a moment, unsure how to continue. Only two weeks had passed since Mike Warren's funeral. Mike had been a career cop with a wife and three kids, well known and well liked. Burying him had been hell.

"So, how long has your son been out there?" Fred asked, anxious to move the subject to something more cheerful than getting shot.

Jen sighed inwardly. Back to homes and gardens.

"How long now, honey?" Chuy asked his wife.

"He and Alicia moved out there in the summer of '86. Remember? It was so hot."

"No, I don't remember. Anyway, it's hot every summer," Chuy replied. "Eighty-six! Boy, that was a long time ago. I didn't realize it had been that long. How old am I now, honey? I've lost count."

Laura wrinkled her brow dramatically and pretended to think. "I don't know for sure, papa. About 470 something?"

"Actually," Chuy said, "that may be pretty close. I know one thing for sure: I'm way too damn old for this business. I think that's why they agreed to retire me early. They figured at the rate I was going, I'd get myself killed and they'd have to pay out the benefits to my widow."

Jen stood and began to clear the dishes. What else could they talk but shop? It was all they had in common.

"So what about you?" Chuy asked. "Did they assign you a new partner?"

"Nope, nothing's happened yet. Actually, I'm still on administrative leave," she answered.

"How come? If there was ever a righteous shooting, that

was it. Those guys downtown are so fucking full of crap."

"Well," Lessing said, "I think they're also doing some damage control within the department. They don't want a reputation here for dirty cops like in New York or L.A. I've heard they plan to review all of Mallory's cases. The D.A. figures his testimony on a lot of them was probably tainted. If it overturns convictions and lets some people out of prison, the D.A. wants to be the one who initiates it, not some journalism student from UTEP. I think the department sees a lot of potential for big time lawsuits and instant loss of credibility if they don't act fast." She finished stacking dishes and turned from the sink.

"They want to keep you away from the press," Chuy pronounced. "Don't want your face on the news."

"You're probably right. Besides," she added, "I haven't decided if I'm going back." There, she thought, she'd finally said it. Stated out loud like that, the idea of quitting didn't sound all that bizarre. She watched the expressions of the three people at the table. The only one who seemed to have any particular reaction was Fred, who was trying—without success—to hide his pleasure.

The couples sat talking for another hour before Chuy pled a need for rest. Shortly afterward, he and his wife headed home. Relieved the gathering had broken up at last, Jen turned to Fred, framing his face in her hands.

"So you're really quitting?" he asked, trying to keep the hope from his voice.

"Let's just say I'm giving the idea some serious consideration. I'm not sure I'm in the business for the right reasons. Care for a drink?" She headed for the bar and Fred followed. "Being in it for the wrong reason is how cops go bad, you know."

"Yeah, I could use a drink," he said. "After the last couple of weeks, I could use several. A scotch on the rocks, since you're mixing."

"I know who killed Davis," Jen said in a matter of fact tone. "Who burned down his house. And who sent me the tape of Mallory's conversations." She turned and faced Fred as she selected the appropriate bottle and removed an ice tray from the refrigerator under the bar.

"Have you told Chuy?" Fred asked after several moments.

"Nope. Don't have to. He already knows. Changed his perception of gays, though. That much I can tell you." The ice in the glass popped softly as she poured the clear brown liquid over it. "I have no proof, really." She handed the glass to Fred.

"So do you plan on doing anything about it?" he asked.

"Nope. To tell you the God's honest truth, I know, but I don't care. That's what's really strange. I realized I didn't really give a rat's ass about what happened to Davis. Or Schneider, even as bad as that was. Or Neal Pearson. Or Mallory. Especially Mallory. I could have killed them all myself, Fred, given the circumstances."

"So who did it?"

"Oh, it's a long story. I'll trot it out for you sometime. Just not tonight. Tonight I need to sit by the pool and listen to the desert. And have a drink with you. If I'm not mistaken, we have some catching up to do."

"Best offer I've had in a while," he said. "I'll bring along the bottle and some ice. Anyway, tomorrow's Sunday."

Jen laughed her girl's laugh as she walked out to the patio. It had been a long time since he'd heard it.

| ✱ |

Little remains of Santos De La O except a birth certificate, a passport, and a few odds and ends of sentimental value residing in a safe deposit box in a San Francisco bank vault. In his new incarnation, he is Alessandro Lanzavecchia, a native of Milano, Italy, a naturalized American citizen, back in the States after time spent abroad, his papers all in order. Alessandro owns a 9-mm pistol, a Sig Sauer, for which he has a concealed carry permit issued by the state of Florida. The gun has never been fired in anger.

He has invested wisely and leads a comfortable, if peripatetic, life. Initial public offerings of biotech companies are his specialty. The company in which he holds the most shares has recently completed clinical trials of Prostagen, an immunomodulator believed to have the potential to eradicate prostate cancer. FDA approval of Immunogen, the company's AIDS vaccine, has driven its stock to previously unheard of heights, creating hundreds of instant millionaires—Alessandro Lanzavecchia chief among them.

Alessandro stands at the open window of his bayside room at the Inn Above Tide and looks out across the darkened water toward the skyline of San Francisco. The clean breath of the sea smells like freshly cut watermelon. He has always regarded the view of the city from the marina in Sausalito as the best. Following the elegant span of the distant Bay bridge, fragile as a cobweb, his eyes move slowly over the glowing silhouette of the city's heart, then to the dark shoulder of the Presidio and out to its right arm, the Golden Gate Bridge, her massive towers shrouded in fog.

Even now, at moments like this, it pleases him to think that in some way he does not understand, Tony can still see through his eyes, his memory insubstantial yet alive. He turns from the window and plucks his jacket from the back of a chair, passing his hands over the supple leather. He will be going into the city tonight, to a restaurant, and later a dance club. Below him in the blackness of the bay, the running lights of boats pass over the water as silently as ghosts in dreams.